The Right Way to Write Christian Fiction

by Tiffany Buckner-Kameni

The Right Way to Write Christian Fiction
Copyright © 2014
Author Tiffany Buckner-Kameni
Email: info@anointedfire.com

Cover design: Anointed Fire™ Christian Publishing
Publisher: Anointed Fire™ Christian Publishing
Publisher's Website: www.afirepublishing.com

ALL RIGHTS RESERVED. This book contains material protected under International and Federal Copyright Laws and Treaties. Any unauthorized reprint or use of this material is prohibited. No part of this book may be reproduced or transmitted in any form or by any means, electronic or mechanical, including photocopying, recording, or by any information storage and retrieval system without express written permission from the author / publisher.

ISBN-13: 978-0692296882 (Anointed Fire)
ISBN-10: 0692296883

You may NOT sell or redistribute this book!

Disclaimer: This book is designed to provide information and motivation to our readers. It is sold with the understanding that the publisher is not engaged to render any type of psychological, legal, or any other kind of professional advice. No warranties or guarantees are expressed or implied by the author, since every man has his own measure of faith. The individual author(s) shall not be liable for any physical, psychological, emotional, financial, or commercial damages, including; but not limited to, special, incidental, consequential or other damages. Our views and rights are the same: You are responsible for your own choices, actions, and results.

The stories in this book are fictional. Names, characters, businesses, places, events and incidents are either the products of the author's imagination or used in a fictitious manner. Any resemblance to actual persons, living or dead, or actual events is purely coincidental.

DEDICATION

TO MY FATHER IN HEAVEN
This book is dedicated to the one and the only
GOD there is: JEHOVAH (YAHWEH). Thank You
for Your love, grace and mercy. I dedicate this
book, everything that I have, and all that I am to
You. Thank You for being an all-present, all-
consuming and loving force in my life. Thank You
for giving me this book, and entrusting me to teach
Your people. I pray that I never let You down. I
love You both privately and publicly, and I will
NEVER be ashamed of You, for You are my Light,
my Rock, my Salvation, my Strong tower, my
Healer, my Safety, my Provider and my Everything.
Let Your Name be magnified in all that I do, and let
Your Name be glorified in all that I say. You,
JEHOVAH, are GOD alone, and I worship,
reverence and adore You.

Table of Contents

Introduction..VII

Should a Christian Write Fiction?..............1

Your Role As a Christian Author..............5

Is Fiction Right For You?...........................13

Your Book's Plot...27

Titling Your Book..63

Characters & Character Dialogues....77

Book Fluffing...95

25 Rules to Write By.................................107

What's Your Writing Style?.....................133

Writing a Best-Seller................................151

Exercising Your Writing Skills................163

Writing Exercises.......................................177

Introduction

Fictional books are pretty popular these days, so it's no wonder that so many Christian authors are throwing their fictitious hats into the ring. Needless to say, writing fiction isn't as simple as starting and ending a story; fictional writing requires passion, research and creativity. Additionally, writing Christian books is remarkably different than writing secular books, but because so many first-time authors are not aware of this fact, they end up writing secular books with religious undertones.

The Right Way to Write Christian Fiction is an instructional guide that details the do's and the don'ts of Christian fictional writing. Filled with story examples and advice, this book will not only show you how to professionally write Christian fiction, but you'll learn the language of fictional writing.

Pair this book up with The Right Way to Write a Christian Book (Parts I & II) for the ultimate writing experience!

Should a Christian Write Fiction?

I know the answer is pretty obvious because I'm writing a book teaching you how to properly write fictional books. But, as a Christian, you will likely get bombarded with questions about whether or not it is acceptable to GOD for Christians to write fictional books. Of course, you want to know how to answer the critics, but at the same time, you want to know if you're in right-standing with GOD. Are you lying when you write stories that you're not sure even happened? The answer is clear: no. There's no new thing underneath the sun, so if you're writing about things that possibly happened, they likely did happen.

CHRIST spoke many parables, and each parable was designed to teach a lesson. Was

Should a Christian Write Fiction?

CHRIST present when each story that HE told occurred? Yes, because HE is the WORD of GOD; meaning, HE is omnipresent (everywhere at the same time). But how does this relate to you? After all, you're not omnipresent; you're only in one place at any given time. It's simple: If the SPIRIT of GOD, which is omnipresent, gives you a story to tell, that story actually did happen somewhere. You may not be familiar with the people or have witnessed that particular story in action, but if you are saved, you have the SPIRIT of GOD residing in you.

Now, of course, it's never good to tell lies. For example, it wouldn't be acceptable to tell stories about space aliens, ghosts, or anything that simply does not exist. It is never good to speak of things that you know never occurred. If you do, you've intentionally told a lie.

When I wrote the book, *Wise Her Still*, my original intention for that book was to make it

Should a Christian Write Fiction?

into a devotional. I wanted to post a few wise quotes and some scriptures; that was the extent of my plans for *Wise Her Still*. Howbeit, GOD had another plan for that book.

I would listen to GOD for wisdom, and I posted whatever wise quote I heard, and then, GOD laid it upon my heart to explain the quote. After explaining the quote, GOD laid it upon my heart to illustrate the quote in story-like fashion. After *Wise Her Still* hit the shelves, I began receiving lots of emails from women who'd read the book, and some of them said they felt as if they were reading the story of their lives. Some said they'd went through exactly what some of the characters went through in *Wise Her Still*, so I began asking women to name their characters in *Wise Her Still*.

Wise Her Still is a compilation of short stories that would be referred to as fictional, but in truth, they are true stories. The only issue is: I didn't personally know the people associated with those stories when I wrote them.

Should a Christian Write Fiction?

To the question: Should a Christian write fiction? Yes, a Christian can write what the world refers to as fiction as long as what they are writing was given to them by GOD.

Your Role As a Christian Author

Many Christian authors, and aspiring Christian authors come on the writing scene confused about their roles. Because of this confusion, many new authors write and publish books that reflect their fears of being criticized. For example, I've come across a lot of books where the authors wrote passively, and they were afraid to touch certain topics because they didn't want to deal with overly sensitive critics. In other words, they wrote their books in the spirit of fear, and not the spirit of faith. As a result, their books were nothing more than powerless stacks of paper that shouted to the readers that the author was a coward. Additionally, fear opens the floodgates for critics looking for platforms.

Your Role As a Christian Author

Fear is a spirit. How do we know this? *"For God hath not given us the spirit of fear; but of power, and of love, and of a sound mind" (2 Timothy 1:7).*

As a writer, you'll notice that anytime you've written something that you know the church may view as controversial, fear will try to raise its ugly head in your heart. You'll want to remove that text, or you may consider editing it to make it less offensive. But telling the truth isn't being offensive; it's delivering a message, and anytime a person does not like the message being delivered, they will take offense. Nevertheless, your role as a writer isn't to make sure that everyone loves you and no one is offended by anything you write. Your role as a Christian author is to deliver the WORD of GOD to the masses. You should always write whatever GOD told you to write in the way that HE told you to write it. Removing or editing the text is the same as watering down your book.

Your Role As a Christian Author

In addition to fear, many Christian authors struggle with self-glorification. Truthfully, we are all souls who struggle to stay in the will of GOD everyday. The difference between a Christian writer and a secular writer is that most Christian authors (not all) write to glorify GOD. Our stories are supposed to draw souls to CHRIST, and they are supposed to help individuals who are struggling in life to lean on the WORD of GOD. But because we struggle with sin, our sinful nature (flesh) is always looking for an opportunity to glorify itself. A perfect example is: I've run across quite a few people who've said to me that GOD had given them a statement or phrase to post online, but they didn't obey HIM because those statements or phrases were catchy. Instead, they said they wanted to keep those quotes for their own upcoming books. In short, they wanted the glory for themselves. They didn't want someone else to take those statements that they felt were their own and capitalize on them.

Your Role As a Christian Author

Years later, they still hadn't written any books or told the world what they said that GOD told them to say. So, why is it hard for them to finally write the books that they claim GOD has told them to write? It's simple. GOD said if you're faithful over little, HE will make you ruler over much. They weren't faithful to GOD; instead, they were determined to get HIS glory all for themselves. If they had written their books in those seasons of disobedience, GOD would not be the main character or subject of their books; they would be their own main characters. Sure, they'd mention HIS name, but their books would be nothing more than secular books disguised as Christian literature. Does this mean that they are bad people who have reserved parking spaces in hell? No. It simply means that they were not yet at a place in their lives where they could be trusted by GOD because anything HE gave them would be seen by them as an opportunity to glorify themselves. This just means that they weren't mature enough to be trusted, therefore, they

Your Role As a Christian Author

weren't trustworthy. They weren't faithful over little, so GOD did not make them ruler over much. GOD knew that they needed more of HIM before they went out to tell the world about HIM. When a person doesn't know a lot about GOD, they can't say much about HIM, so they'll talk about the one person they know the most about: themselves.

Anytime you write a book, your flesh will always try to find some sort of way to insert itself into that book, but you have to be willing to remove any pointless or self-glorifying information that you come across. If you don't, many of your readers will see right through you, and your book won't reach best-seller status. Remember, when people buy Christian books, they are looking for answers and clean entertainment; they aren't looking for you. That's why we have to always be aware of our own motives whenever we write books or attach the word "Christian" to our books.

Your Role As a Christian Author

When writing your book, it is always a good idea to reread the book, and if you find any sentences, paragraphs, or pages you're uncomfortable with, either revise or delete them.

For every paragraph, ask yourself: Is GOD glorified? Will my readers be encouraged by what I've written? Will my readers learn from what I've written? Does this paragraph add value to my book, or does it take away from the book itself? Believe it or not, a few bad sentences can single-handedly destroy an entire book, and one bad book can single-handedly destroy an author's writing career. General rule of thumb: If a sentence doesn't add to your book, it takes away from your book.

Anytime a story is good, you may find yourself getting lost in that story, but when a story isn't so good, you'll feel rushed to end it. For this reason, you should never continue writing a story that you don't like. Many authors start off

Your Role As a Christian Author

writing boring stories with the hopes that those stories will get better along the way. Once they've gotten into the heart of those stories and found that the stories were still boring, they didn't want to delete them because they'd invested a lot of time into writing them. After that, the authors began to tell themselves that maybe the stories were good, but because they are the authors, they may have been a little prejudiced. Needless to say, if you don't like the story, your readers probably won't like the story.

Your role as a Christian author is simple: Glorify GOD with your book. Take the lessons you've learned in life, and the lessons you've learned through CHRIST, and teach others through them. It's not that difficult to be a Christian author; you simply cannot give in to public pressure. There will be a lot of people who will call your writings offensive, but your assignment isn't to answer the critics. GOD assigned you to winning and restoring souls to

Your Role As a Christian Author

CHRIST. GOD will handle the critics. Your assignment requires that you be bold and selfless, not cowardly and selfish. Pay attention to most Christian best-sellers. They didn't acquire their best-seller status by pacifying their audiences; they attained and maintained faithful readers by being bold enough to shake up their readers' realities with the truth. GOD is bold, and HE has one of the best-selling books out ever known, and it's called the Holy Bible. If you let HIM be your coach, HE will take you places in your writing career that most authors will never go and have never been.

Is Fiction Right For You?

Let's face it: Writing a fictional book is definitely not for everyone. Fictional writing requires a lot of details, thoughts, and paced writing. Most people don't stop to smell the flowers, and people who never pay attention to the details in life usually aren't very good with writing, especially writing fictional books.

Fictional writing is very different than non-fictional writing. An author writing a self-help book only needs to convey their advice to the readers; whereas, a person writing a fictional book has to convey their advice through story-telling. Fictional writing has more depth than non-fictional writing because it illustrates a story through the use of words, while conveying a message through that story. Read the story below and see if you can identify

Is Fiction Right For You?

what's wrong with it:

Jacob was walking home from school when two special-ed children came out of a crowd in his direction. He knew they were coming to fight him. Jacob was scared, and he hoped the boys wouldn't hit him. Suddenly, one of the boys hit Jacob and knocked him unconscious.
----*End of example.*

There are many things wrong with this story. First, it doesn't tell the reader why the children hit Jacob. Secondly, the boys who hit Jacob are obviously an important part of the story; therefore, their names should be mentioned. Next, there aren't many details given, and the story reads as if it was being told by a first-grader. Lastly, what's the reason for stating that the children who hit Jacob are in special education?

The truth is, many authors write stories in the same manner as the story above was written. I'll venture out to say that most authors who attempt to write Christian fictional books write

Is Fiction Right For You?

their stories in the same manner as the story above was written. There is little to no detail added, and there is an abundance of useless information that's not going to add to the story. Let's rewrite the story in a more professional way:

Jacob's stomach was in knots as he watched the clock. It was almost three o'clock in the afternoon, and school would be letting out soon. Ordinarily, Jacob was happy when school was out, but today was different. Today, he'd made fun of two boys that were in special education classes.

Earlier, Jacob had seen Raymond and Patrick in the cafeteria, and because the two boys were ordinarily quiet, Jacob thought it would be a good idea to make fun of them.

"Hey, Raymond and Patrick! I just got a call that your classroom was on fire, and they said to tell all remedial students to leave your lunch trays with me and go back to the classroom so you can drool on the fire!" screamed Jacob.

Is Fiction Right For You?

The cafeteria erupted with laughter as Jacob began to make fun of Raymond and Patrick.

Jacob didn't know that Raymond and Patrick were brothers who were known for their "fists of steel", as some students would say. Jacob was a new student attempting to make a name for himself, and he'd crossed the line. While in the cafeteria, one of the brothers had walked up to Jacob and patted him on the shoulder. "See you after school," said Patrick. "I can't wait to drool on you."
The laughter stopped as the children realized that today's comedy session would end in a fight, and they'd get to see Raymond and Patrick pound yet another bully.
"One-Two-Three, come on," said Drake Williams, a sophomore who was also in special education. "I know which way he walks home."
Jacob was confused. Why had everyone stopped laughing, and why had Drake Williams referred to Patrick as "One-Two-Three?"
Curious, Jacob turned to Stephen. Stephen

Is Fiction Right For You?

had been one of the boys who'd been instigating the confrontation. "Why did he call him One-Two-Three?," asked Jacob. Stephen answered with, "Because, he hits his foes three times, and they are always knocked out between the first and the third punch."

Jacob kept thinking about the events that had transpired in the cafeteria earlier. Why hadn't someone warned him about Patrick and Raymond? Suddenly, the sound that Jacob dreaded pierced the silence. It was the sound of the school's bell, but to Jacob, it was the sound of impending doom.

Jacob lagged behind as the other students left the classroom one by one, celebrating the start of the weekend. He kept trying to think of ways that he could get out of the fight. He thought about taking the long way home; he thought about staying on school grounds, and he even thought about calling the police. Nevertheless, nothing seemed more dreadful than the idea of

Is Fiction Right For You?

looking like a coward.

Jacob grabbed his books and loaded them into his backpack. He slowly walked out of the classroom, and was relieved to see the hallways were now almost empty. It seemed that he'd stayed behind just long enough to thwart off the impending fight. He walked out of the school and started heading home.

As Jacob neared the street he lived on, he saw what looked like the entire school gathered around in a huddle.
Jacob's heart raced as he approached the crowd. Maybe he'd win the fight after all. Maybe there would be no fight. After all, it seemed as if the crowd was distracted by something, and Jacob hoped they were gathered to watch another fight.
Another fight would prove to be just the distraction that a scared Jacob would need to make his escape. Suddenly, a voice rang out. "There he is!" shouted a little girl who couldn't

Is Fiction Right For You?

be anymore than eight years old. As it turned out, the children had gathered together to make bets on how many punches it would take to knock Jacob out.

Jacob's heart dropped as Raymond and Patrick emerged from the crowd. Suddenly, Patrick looked taller and more intimidating as he approached the now frozen Jacob. He'd removed his school shirt, revealing a somewhat dirty tank top and bulging muscles. Jacob's mind raced as he attempted to decide his next move. Should he stay and fight or should he run? Should he beg for his life or should he remain silent? He could feel his guts churning as Raymond and Patrick approached him.

"To be fair, you'll be fighting me only," said Patrick. "After I knock you out, my brother and I are going to drool over your stiff body." Patrick appeared confident, and it was obvious that he was going to enjoy knocking Jacob out. The smirk on his face was overridden by the anger in his eyes.

Is Fiction Right For You?

Jacob opened his mouth to apologize, but the words wouldn't come out. Suddenly, Patrick swung at Jacob with his right hand, and Jacob reacted quickly by blocking the shot, but he wasn't prepared for what happened next. As it turned out, the right hand was just a distraction, and as Jacob blocked Patrick's right hand, he saw Patrick's left fist before it met his face.

The punch was so intense that Jacob lost consciousness immediately. He was awakened by laughter and the sounds of the children chanting, "One-Two-Three...One-Two-Three...One-Two-Three!" As Jacob began regaining consciousness, he could feel something warm and wet drizzling down his face. Patrick and Raymond had honored their word; they'd drooled on Jacob's stiff body.

The crowd laughed and Jacob could see some of the children exchanging money. One guy could be heard saying that he had been the only one who'd bet that Jacob would be

Is Fiction Right For You?

knocked out with one punch. Jacob wanted to lift his head, but he was too ashamed and too dazed to move. He kept feeling a tugging on his body. A couple of the guys were trying to stand him on his feet.

----*End of example.*

As you'll notice, the second rendition of the story is a lot longer and more detailed than the first. That's because writing is an art form, and should never be rushed through. Your readers will want details, and if you can't fathom the idea of taking such a short story and extending that story to give it more details and more depth, then fictional (creative) writing is just not for you.

The average author will try to take a scene and sum it up in a few words, because the average author has a point they want to make, and they want to get to that point quickly. But the average reader wants to be taken into the situation, and they want to experience that

Is Fiction Right For You?

situation. Readers want to feel, see and experience what your main character feels, sees and experiences. Your readers will live vicariously through the main character. In the story above, the readers will see themselves as opponents of Jacob. They will experience his fear; they will experience his humiliation, and they will enjoy his fall.

Fictional writing isn't just telling a story; it's creating an atmosphere for your story to be told. So, is fictional writing for you? Check out the pointers below.

1. **Are you an avid reader?** Reading a lot of books will not only prepare you for your career as a fictional writer, but it'll help you to experience the emotions that you want your readers to experience. You'll notice how each story brings you in, and you'll notice how they make you feel with each turn of the page. That's what you want your readers to experience. Always read a

Is Fiction Right For You?

lot of fictional books to prepare yourself for your writing journey.

2. **Do you pay attention to details?** Good writers are oftentimes very analytical, and will notice what appears to be some of life's most minute details. For example, good writers will oftentimes stop and study a bumblebee on a flower. Good writers will oftentimes know the names of the flowers, the behaviors of the bees, and the climates they thrive best in. That's because creative writers often analyze everything; whereas, not-so-good writers are oftentimes very fast-paced and seem to rush through life. Take the time out to study the rust on a gate, the sound of lightning, or the smell of grass on a rainy day. Such details make for good writing.

3. **Are you well-traveled?** Believe it or not, most best-selling authors who've written fictional books have traveled to

Is Fiction Right For You?

other countries. If you're always around the same people within the same communities, your writing will be limited to what and who you know. This means that all of your characters will sound and behave the same, and you'll limit your audience. Get out and travel more. Writing is more than just writing; it's being able to take a story, and tell it in a way that people from many walks of life can understand and relate to.

4. **Have you lived a little?** Great writers are oftentimes people who've experienced more drama in life than average people. Living in a small town, going to the same job and experiencing the same things day-to-day is not the recipe for good writing. People who've done things that most people have never done, and have experienced things that most people have never experienced are usually better at creating fictional books than people who

Is Fiction Right For You?

haven't experienced a lot.

5. **Are you patient?** In this book, you'll notice how a story that's nothing more than a few sentences long is expanded to several paragraphs or several pages. Good writing requires a lot of patience and a lot of attention to detail. If you're not patient, and you'd rather hurry through a story, you may want to consider writing children's books, plays, or short articles. Fictional writing, at its best, is descriptive.

When I moved to Florida, I was amazed at the amount of Floridians who didn't know the names of the different birds that perched in front of their homes daily. They'd been living in Florida all of their lives, and their knowledge of their feathery neighbors was limited to whether the birds were pests or not.
Every time I saw a large bird, I'd make a mental note to research the bird and learn what type of bird it was. I'd research its behaviors,

Is Fiction Right For You?

its mating rituals, what it preyed on, and what preyed on it.

Anytime I would mention the name of a bird to a native Floridan, I would be surprised when they'd ask me what it was called again. Now, if I were to meet someone who knew the birds and their behaviors, I could almost guarantee you that they'd be writers or aspiring writers. Again, writers are analytical and will oftentimes be found conducting research on whatever it is that grasps their attention.

Your Book's Plot

Every fictional book must have a plot. Reference.com defines "plot" as: *The plan, scheme, or main story of a literary or dramatic work, as a play, novel, or short story.*

Basically, your book's plot is whatever your book is about. The plot of your book is the challenges that the main character or characters will find themselves having to face. What's the story behind your story? What messages are you trying to convey in your book? If you're the main character, what obstacles are you facing and what is it that you're trying to achieve? Anytime an author writes a book with no plot, that author has written a book with no basis. What is the main character's purpose, and how do you want your readers to feel about the main character?

Your Book's Plot

Asking yourself these questions is important, because your answers will show up in your book. If you're unsure of the book's plot, you need to take a step back and develop your story mentally, taking time out to jot down some notes, before committing your story to paper or to the internet.

A book with no storyline is oftentimes written by a person who simply wants the author title, but does not want to do the work associated with becoming an author. For this reason, self-publishing has gotten a bad reputation. As an author, you want to make sure that you are labeled and recognized as a genuine author; someone who loves to write and has taken time out to think of a story that would not only engage the readers, but teach and entertain those readers. Check out the storyline below.

Angela's heart raced as the judge called her up to testify. It was her time to tell her side of the story, and she was petrified.

Your Book's Plot

Angela stood to her feet and made her way to the witness stand. With every step, she could hear her heart racing. Nevertheless, she knew that if Trent was to be declared not guilty by reason of insanity, he would come after her until she was dead. Angela wiped her palms on her skirt as she neared the stand.

It felt as if the walk had taken forever. She stopped as she neared the stand, and placed her hands on her swollen belly. Her little boy was due to be born any day now, and Angela wanted to make sure that his monstrous father would not be free to torment her or her new baby, a baby in which she'd initially planned to abort.

As she turned to face the audience, her eyes immediately met with Trent's eyes. Nervous, Angela froze as he blew a kiss in her direction. Did he not realize the seriousness of what he'd done? Did he not realize that he was facing twenty-five years to life on the charges of kidnapping, rape, assault with a deadly

Your Book's Plot

weapon, and arson?

After being sworn in, Angela sat down and tried to keep her eyes off Trent as the Prosecutor began his line of questioning.

----*End of example.*

So far, what we've gathered from this story is that Angela is in court, and her ex-boyfriend likely kidnapped, raped, and assaulted her. He then set something on fire, but we don't understand what or why. Telling readers about a problem without getting to the root of the problem could take what could potentially be a good story and make it bad. Now, let's get to the root of Angela's story.

Angela remembered that dreadful day with amazing clarity. It was raining outside one Sunday morning and Angela was just beginning to wake up from a sound sleep. The sound of the rain was so comforting that Angela considered spending the rest of her day in bed. Nevertheless, Angela knew she

Your Book's Plot

needed to catch up on a lot of work before she returned to work that following Monday.

Angela sighed and stretched, and without warning, her leg touched what felt like another person's leg behind her. How could that be? She lived alone, and her daughter was spending the summer with her father hours away in Pennsylvania. Petrified, Angela slowly turned her head and was horrified at what she saw. Behind her lay her ex-boyfriend Trent Marsallis.

She thought hard and long, and suddenly remembered that she had been out at a local club the night before. She'd been hanging out with her best friend Tara, and the two ladies had spent the night drinking whatever they could get their hands on. The last memory that Angela could recall was asking Tara to hold her drink while she went to dance with a new face that was in the club that night. That was it. Angela couldn't remember anymore about that night.

Your Book's Plot

Trent appeared to be sleeping, so Angela tried to slip out of bed unnoticed, but Trent's almost girl-like voice broke the silence.

"Good morning, beautiful," he said. "I knew you missed me, but I didn't know you missed me that much."

Angela froze. She had a restraining order on Trent. Trent and Angela had dated more than three years ago, and Trent had spent the last three years making Angela's life a living nightmare. He'd attacked her at a local supermarket, attempted to kidnap her from a mutual friend's house, and broken her car and house windows several times. He'd even gotten her fired from one of her jobs. He'd only served a maximum of three days in jail for his crimes against her because the investigators could never gather up enough evidence to prove that he was the culprit behind all of the break-ins. Additionally, Trent was cunning. He'd always told investigators that he and Angela were just having a lover's spat, and that

Your Book's Plot

they would reconcile by the end of the day as they always did. It seemed that his lies had worked. Many officers stopped taking Angela's calls seriously, even after Trent had attempted to kidnap her. He'd told officers that Angela had drank too much liquor that night, and he was just trying to get her in his car to take her home, since she was well over the blood-alcohol limit, and officers believed him. After all, Angela was a party girl, and she was known around town for her drunken outbursts.

"Trent. How did you get in my house?" asked Angela. "You know I have a restraining order out on you." Trent rubbed his hands through Angela's hair. His hands wreaked of oil and what smelled like decomposing flesh, and his breath wasn't any friendlier.

"Angela, don't act like that. I saw you in the club and you were drunk. I saw Tara too, but she'd left with some guy, so I offered to take you home and you agreed. When we got back to your place, you couldn't keep your hands off me, so it's safe to say that we're back together again. I'm happy. Aren't you happy?"

Trent's breath was repulsive, and even though Angela still had her back to him, she could smell Trent's rotten teeth. It was obvious that the rumors about Trent were true. After Angela and Trent's breakup, Trent had slipped deeper and deeper into mental illness, and he'd stopped taking care of himself.

Angela was too afraid to turn and look at Trent. What had she done? She attempted to speak calmly to Trent because she knew that he was mentally unstable.

Angela: Trent, we're not back together, and I'm not sure how you got in my house. If you leave now, I won't call the police. I don't know what happened between us, but understand that we are not back together.

Trent: Angela, what are you talking about, baby? We are back together and ain't no restraining order, court order, or police officer gonna keep us apart anymore. Not even the

Your Book's Plot

judge! We put all that foolishness behind us last night, so just come back to bed and let's make the best of our relationship.

Angela: We don't have a relationship. It's over between you and I. It's been over between us for three years now... remember? I don't want you back. Please leave my house, and I will not call the police this time. Please just leave.

Trent: Baby? Guess what? Do you remember our song? I recorded it on a CD and I want to play it for you again. It's still in the radio from last night.

Angela: Trent, please leave my house. I'm asking you nicely.

Trent: Guess what else? I got your name tattooed on my shoulder. Look.

Angela: Trent! For the last time, leave my house before I call the police! I've asked you nicely, and I've even said I won't press charges on you for violating the restraining order. Please leave!

Trent looked at Angela as he calmly sat up in

Your Book's Plot

the bed. Tears began to fall from his eyes, and he began to rock back and forth. The realization began to sit in yet again. Angela didn't want him, even though he wanted her.

Trent: I've fought hard for you, Angie!
Angela: Trent...
Trent: No! Shut up! I've fought hard for you. I fought against all those people who were trying to break us up! I fought with my family and now I don't have anywhere to stay! I fought with the police and they took me to jail! I fought with the judge and he kept sending me to jail again and again and again! And for what? Because I love you! I keep getting arrested in the name of love! But you don't love me back!

Without a warning, Trent suddenly struck Angela with so much force that she fell face-down on the floor. Angela turned her body over and began to plead with Trent as he hovered over her. Angela was still hung over

Your Book's Plot

from the night before, and the alcohol in her blood made it difficult for her to fight back.

Trent's eyes were dark. Suddenly, his rotten teeth and putrid breath were the least of Angela's problems. She tried to push him off her, but every time she resisted him, Trent would hit her even harder than the previous time.

"If you can't love me, I'll make you die. You will die today because you didn't love me!" Trent's tears fell in Angela's face as he repeated his deadly words again and again while striking her repeatedly. "You're dying today, Angela!" Angela was too weak to put up a good fight. She couldn't fight back and she couldn't overpower him, so she stopped resisting what she knew Trent was attempting to do. He was about to rape her and she knew it.

After the rape was over, Trent continued to berate Angela with words. "You were my everything, Angie! I would have done anything

Your Book's Plot

for you... Do you hear me? Anything! But you sent the police after me, and I know why the judge kept sending me to jail. You were sleeping with him, weren't you, Angie? Say it! Say it!"

Angela was still on the floor, and by this time, Trent had his hands around her neck. "I didn't sleep with him," Angela managed to muster out. "I don't even know the man." Angela's words infuriated Trent even more, and he began to strike her repeatedly.

"You're going to die today, Angela," said Trent. "You're going to die because you didn't love me, but I loved you."

Trent choked Angela until she blacked out. When she came to, Trent was gone and her house was on fire.

A wrench rested next to Angela's body, and as she regained her eyesight, she could tell that the wrench had been used to strike her because it was covered in blood. As she attempted to stand to her feet, she immediately

Your Book's Plot

fell back down. Her body was weak, and the smell of the smoke had begun to overpower her.

Angela dragged her body towards her nightstand so she could grab her phone, but the smoke was too much for her. She could feel herself losing consciousness once again. As she opened her eyes, she could see what appeared to be a beautiful angel standing over her.

Was this it? Was this how she was going to die: Raped, beaten, bruised, drunk and confused? Suddenly, Angela heard what sounded like a walkie-talkie. She tried to open her mouth, but no words would come out. That's when everything went dark again.

The light was just too bright. Angela tried to open her eyes, but the migraine headache was overwhelming. She could hear beeping sounds, but she couldn't recognize where she was. Suddenly, a man's face appeared over her.

Your Book's Plot

"Ms. Dawson, can you hear me? If you can hear me, squeeze my hand."

Why couldn't she do it? Why couldn't she squeeze the man's hand? That's when it dawned on Angela. She wasn't in Heaven, and she wasn't in hell; she was at the hospital.

----*End of example.*

Now, we have a plot.

What's the problem?

There are two problems in this story. Of course, Trent is a big problem, and Angela is a problem to herself. Her partying has placed her in harm's way yet again.

Where's the struggle?

The story is short, but if told in more detail, it would have to give detailed accounts of Trent stalking Angela. Readers would also like to be taken inside the relationship between Trent and Angela when it appeared to be a good relationship. Readers would want to see the deterioration of their relationship, the deterioration of Trent's mental health, and the

Your Book's Plot

escalation of Trent's stalking.

What (unsuccessful) attempts were made to resolve the problems?

In almost every good book, you will see several attempts made by the main characters to avoid problems and to resolve problems, but those efforts proved to be futile. Angela attempted to resolve her problem with Trent first by reasoning with him, then by having him arrested, and finally, by getting a restraining order against him. None of those efforts proved to be useful with Trent. So now, the readers are all disgusted with Trent and anxious to see what's going to happen to him. The final court appearance would be the peak of this book, and in court, we'd have to introduce some problems to make it appear that Trent just may get off after all. After that, we'd have to introduce a hero to excite the readers.

In this case, we could cause Trent's mother to be a hero because it is unlikely that a mother would testify against her son. We could cause

Your Book's Plot

Tara to spring up and become the hero, even though we'd have to show that before the court session began that Angela was mad at Tara. We could even cause Trent to be the villain and the hero by penciling in that he had a change of heart and felt awful for what he'd done to Angela.

What is the resolution?

It's a Christian book designed to teach a lesson, so we definitely can't give in to public pressure. Most people would want us to kill Trent with our pencils. Sure, we could kill Trent, but this wouldn't necessarily glorify GOD. We could send Trent to prison for the rest of his life, or we could cause Trent to hang himself in his cell. We could even set ourselves up for a part two by having Trent escape from prison. At the same time, most people would want Angela to abort her baby because it was Trent's baby, but again, we are Christian authors and we should always tell the story the way GOD would want the story told. Sure, GOD doesn't want us raped, beaten and

Your Book's Plot

left for dead, but should anything like that happen to someone, we are responsible for conveying a message to that person through the books GOD has entrusted us to write. Either way, we have to introduce a resolution, one that most readers would be pleased with, but at the same time, one that GOD will be pleased with.

Angela would need to repent of her ways, get into a Bible-based church, and submit her life to the LORD. We could then take Angela and show her years later as an evangelist or as an advocate for victims of domestic abuse. We could grow Angela's new baby boy up as a loving and supportive son who's fully aware of how he was conceived. The point is: We have to introduce a problem, a series of attempts to resolve that problem, a resolution and a hero. Additionally, not only do we have to show a problem, we must show an escalation of that problem. We can even show what initially appeared to be a successful solving of the problem, only to have that resolution itself lead

Your Book's Plot

to the escalation of the problem.

Finally, your readers will want to know the entire story. What happened to Tara? Why did Tara allow Angela to leave the club with Trent? As the author of this story, I would have the power to turn Tara into a green-eyed villain who secretly envied and hated Angela, or I could cause the readers to be sympathetic of Tara. Read the alternative endings below and determine which ending you'd prefer.

Alternative Ending One

It was finally Tara's time to take the stand, and it was no surprise that she was seated on the side of the defense team. Ever since the incident, Angela hadn't heard from her, even though Angela had many unanswered questions about Tara's behavior.

Tara stood to her feet and approached the witness stand. She wore a dark blue blazer and a pleated white skirt. Her navy blue pumps perfectly accented the navy leather belt

Your Book's Plot

that clung to her tiny waist. Tara's new haircut made her appear to be somewhat older and more mature. It appeared that she'd went to great lengths to appear as a credible witness. She wanted Trent to beat the charges; after all, she was in love with Trent's brother, Malcolm, and she wasn't too fond of Angela. Truthfully, she hated Angela and everything that Angela stood for.

As Tara entered the stand, she readjusted her blazer and greeted the judge before raising her hand to be sworn out. Angela stared at her former best friend in dismay.
Tara's face was covered in makeup. She didn't look like her usual self. Tara was tomboyish, and hated wearing makeup, dresses, or heels. The smirk on Tara's face almost made Angela nauseous. How could she not have known that Tara envied her? Now, Tara was sitting in the stands wearing an outfit almost identical to what Angela had worn when they'd went to church together, and her new haircut was

Your Book's Plot

similar to the haircut Angela once wore religiously.

Tara looked at Angela and smiled as the line of questioning begin. According to Tara's testimony, Angela had insisted on leaving the club with Trent that night. She'd asked Angela if she was sure about leaving with Trent, but Angela had insisted that she loved him and that they were just going to go back to her place to talk.
 As Tara testified, Angela leaned in and whispered in the Prosecutor's ear. She was outraged at the lies Tara was telling and the extent Tara would go to see her wiped off the face of this earth. Finally, it was the prosecution's turn to cross examine Tara, and the Prosecutor was all too excited about going after her.

Prosecutor: State your name for the record again.

Tara: My name is Tara Renee Madison.

Prosecution: Isn't it true, Ms. Madison, that

Your Book's Plot

you were once best friends with the victim,
Angela Dawson?

Tara: Yes, that's true.

Prosecution: You guys weren't just friends,
now were you? You were best friends. Am I
correct?

Tara: Yes, we were.

Prosecution: Ms. Madison, who is Malcolm
Marsallis?

Tara: *Clears throat.* He's just a friend.

Prosecution: Need I remind you, Ms.
Madison, that you're under oath? Let me ask
you again. Who is Malcolm Marsallis?

Tara: He's my boyfriend. He's Trent's brother,
too.

Prosecution: I think you've left out something.

*The Prosecutor turned to the judge and
handed him a document.*

Prosecutor: Let the records reflect that I am
entering Exhibit A, a marriage license obtained
by Malcolm Marsallis and Tara Madison. So,

Your Book's Plot

Ms. Madison. Let me ask you that question one more time. Who is Malcolm Marsallis to you?

Tara: He's my fiance and he's Trent's brother.

Prosecutor: Your fiance? And isn't it true that on the night of December 15th, 2013, you were at the club with the victim, Angela Dawson?

Tara: Yes, we were at the club together.

Prosecutor: According to your testimony, Ms. Dawson willingly left the club with Mr. Trent Marsallis. Is that correct?

Tara: Yes.

Prosecutor: I have a copy of the original police report in my hand.

The Prosecutor turned to the judge and handed him one copy of the report, and he placed another copy of the report in front of Tara.

Prosecutor: Read for the court what you said in your original statement.

Tara: *Sighs.* Angela was wasted and I was

Your Book's Plot

helping her to her car when Trent approached us. He offered to help me put Angela in the car, and at first, I said no, but Trent was insistent. Trent's brother came to the car and offered to help as well.

We put Angela in the passenger's seat of her car, and Malcolm (Trent's brother) told me to let Trent drive Angela home. He said he wanted to talk to me, and at first, I said no, but he kept telling me that Trent was a changed man. He said that Trent wouldn't hurt Angela and that he'd take me by the house to check on Angela in an hour or so. He then started telling me that he liked me, and while we were talking, Trent was backing Angela's car out with Angela passed out in the passenger's seat. I insisted on following them, but Malcolm wouldn't let me. He said that Angela had been secretly sleeping with Trent, but she had been too ashamed to tell me.

Prosecutor: So, today, your story has changed. What happened, Tara?

Tara: I decided to tell the truth; that's all.

Your Book's Plot

Prosecutor: So, it's your sworn statement here that you were lying to the police?

Tara: I was a little drunk that night, so....

Prosecutor: You were drunk? But you weren't too drunk to remember detail by detail of what you said happened that night! Ms. Madison, why do you hate Angela so much?!

Tara: I don't hate her, but...

Prosecutor: You don't like her, do you?

Tara: What does that have to do with anything?

Prosecutor: Answer the question! Do you like Ms. Dawson?

Tara: *Pauses.* No, I don't like her.

Prosecutor: Isn't it true that you're jealous of Ms. Dawson? As a matter of fact, didn't you tell a police officer that Angela deserved what she got?

Tara: No, I...

Prosecutor: Answer the question, Ms. Madison! Did you or did you not tell a police officer that Angela deserved being attacked, raped, and left for dead? You're under oath, Ms. Madison!

Your Book's Plot

Tara: She did deserve it! She thinks she's better than everyone! Look at her! Sitting there with that innocent look on her face! Trent loved her, and she was too stupid to see it! Why? Because she thinks she's better than everyone else! She thinks the world and everyone in it revolves around her! I got word for you, Ms. Angela. You are no better than Trent! I just wish Trent would've made sure you were dead before he left the house!
Prosecutor: No further questions, Your Honor.
----End of example.

Of course, if we were to write this story in its entirety, we'd have to add some objections from the Defense Attorney, some statements from the Judge, some of Trent's reactions, some of Angela's reactions, and some of the jury's reactions. This would make the story appear more authentic and bring the readers directly into the courtroom that the author has created. Let's review alternative ending number two.

Your Book's Plot

Alternative Ending Two

Tara rose to her feet when she was called to testify. Dressed in a professional blue blazer, a white pleated skirt, and blue pumps, Tara almost didn't look like herself. She was a tomboy, and hated wearing dresses, heels, makeup, or purses.

Tara turned to look at Angela as she approached the witness stand, but Angela wouldn't lift her head to look at Tara.
Sure, Tara was there to testify on Angela's behalf, but Angela was still angry. After all, she hadn't heard from Tara since the incident, and she didn't know why Tara had let her leave with Trent.

Tara walked to the stand and raised her hand to be sworn in. Her makeup made her almost unrecognizable, but it was obvious that she had been crying. Her eyeliner was smeared and her voice strained, so the Prosecutor handed Tara a tissue before proceeding with

Your Book's Plot

his line of questioning.

Prosecutor: State your name for the record again.

Tara: My name is Tara Renee Madison.

Prosecution: Isn't it true, Ms. Madison, that you were once best friends with the victim, Angela Dawson?

Tara: Yes, that's true.

Prosecution: You guys weren't just friends, now were you? You were best friends. Am I correct?

Tara: Yes, we were.

Prosecution: Ms. Madison, what happened on the night of December 15th, 2013.

Tara: Angela and I were at the Banana Peel. It's a nightclub on eleventh street in Manhattan. Well, we were both drunk, but Angela was wasted. We were sitting down in one of the booths, and Angela was pretty much passed out. That's when Malcolm Marsallis approached me.

Tara started crying, and the Prosecutor handed

Your Book's Plot

her a tissue.

Prosecutor: It's okay, Ms. Madison. Take your time.

Tara: I had always had a crush on Malcolm, and he knew it. I mean, I'd told almost everyone. I didn't see Trent, though. I didn't know that Trent was in the club, because you rarely saw Trent and Malcolm together. They were as different as night and day.

Prosecutor: And then what happened?

Tara: Malcolm asked me to dance, but I told him that I couldn't because I needed to keep an eye on Angela. There was another girl sitting at the table, and Malcolm asked her if she would sit with Angela while he and I went to dance, and she agreed. Well, the way the club is made, the dance floor is in a different room than the seating area. I went to the other room, and Malcolm and I danced through three songs.

Tara began to cry uncontrollably as she turned

Your Book's Plot

to look at Angela.

Tara: When I came back, you were gone! The girl said that some guy had come and said that he was your brother!

Prosecutor: It's okay. Speak to me, Ms. Madison. Take a few breaths and calm down.

Tara: Okay. The girl said that some guy had approached the table and said he was Angela's brother, Ricky. I didn't think too much about it because Ricky did come to that club sometimes, and he was always on Angela's case about her partying. The girl told me that Ricky had picked up Angela and said he was taking her home. I was somewhat relieved because I didn't know how I was going to get Angela out of the club that night. She was just too wasted. But I wanted to be sure, so when I left the club, I drove by Angela's house and her car was in the driveway.

Prosecutor: Were there any other cars in the driveway, Ms. Madison?

Tara: No. Angela's car was the only car in the

driveway, so I thought the girl had told the truth. I went up to the house and knocked on the door, but no one answered. I called Angela's phone, but no one answer, so I assumed that she was asleep.

Prosecutor: Take your time. And then, what happened?

Tara: I went home. I didn't have Ricky's number and I knew he didn't have a car, so I assumed he had gotten a ride to the club like he always did and he'd seen his sister passed out. Ricky has always been very protective of Angela. The next day, I got a phone call from another friend saying Angela was in the hospital.

Tara turned to look at Angela again.

Tara: I went to the hospital to visit you, but your family was so mad at me that they wouldn't let me see you! I called your phone when you got out of the hospital, but you'd changed your number! I even went by your house, but it was

Your Book's Plot

still surrounded by police crime scene tape, and the officers there said that you'd moved in with your brother, Ricky. I didn't know Angela and I'm sorry! Please forgive me! I feel like it's my fault. I shouldn't have let Malcolm trick me into leaving you alone!

----*End of example.*

Now, with alternative ending number two, the readers come to understand that Tara wasn't the bad guy in the scenario. She'd been tricked into leaving her best friend with a stranger, only to have Trent come in and kidnap Angela. That's what your readers will want to hear. They will want explanations. You can't leave any stones unturned, otherwise, your readers leave not knowing the whole story.

Which ending would you prefer? Your desired ending tells you a lot about yourself as a person, and it also sheds light into the style of writing you're most prone to. For example, if

Your Book's Plot

you prefer that Tara be the envious friend who wanted to see her best friend killed, you're more likely to write books where the villains are trusted loved ones. This would likely indicate that you've seen your share of betrayal. But if you prefer the second ending, it's likely because you love happy endings. You've probably experienced betrayal, but on a lighter scale than the person who prefers Tara to be a villain. Your stories wouldn't be as deep and revelatory as someone who prefers alternative ending one, but your stories would likely be what some refer to as "feel-good" stories.

The person who prefers alternative ending number one would likely write books that were longer and more in depth because they'd have to explain away Tara's betrayal; meaning, the story couldn't end in the courtroom. Tara would now be a villain, and the readers would have to get a better glimpse at Tara's life as well as see Tara get punished for her role in Angela's attack. The point is: The book has to have a plot that builds upon itself. Just telling a story

Your Book's Plot

will not do you any good if the story has no lesson behind it. In the story of Angela, readers will want to see:

1. Angela give up partying and commit herself to the LORD. Remember, you're a Christian writer, not a secular writer. This means that GOD is to be glorified in your book.

2. Angela give her life to the LORD.

3. Trent be punished for attacking Angela. Readers will also want to see that Trent will not be able to hurt Angela again. You'd have to give Trent a life sentence in prison, give him a short sentence, but have him killed while in prison, or you'd have to cause him to take his own life. That's the harsh reality. Your readers will see Trent as unchangeable, and therefore, they will want to rid Angela's life of him. You can also give him twenty-five years to life, and have him rededicate his life to the LORD. The pen is in your hand to do with Trent as

Your Book's Plot

you so please.

4. An explanation for Tara's behavior that dreadful night.

5. If alternative ending number two was enacted, readers will want to hear from Angela's brother, Ricky.

6. Angela and Trent's son grow up. Readers will be curious as to how he turns out.

Now, for some people, having to go into so many details and stretch a story out as I've done with Angela's story, or any of the stories in this book, would be too much. That's because writing is an art form, and some people just aren't gifted to write. Being able to put together a few words does not automatically qualify someone as a writer. When writing a book, you have to be creative, patient, and passionate.

Remember, your book's plot is the heartbeat of your book, and without it, your book will be as

Your Book's Plot

lifeless as a shoe box. People don't want to just read a story; they want to be moved by that story and encouraged to make changes to their own lives. An author without a plot is an author without a plan. Make sure that your book has layers and layers of details, revelations, and useful information that your readers can bring with them into their own lives.

Titling Your Book

What should you entitle your book? That's the question many new authors are faced with at this very moment. Most authors have at least two to three titles they are considering for their books, and oftentimes, the titles they really want are the ones they've had for quite some time. The problem with using those titles is that their book's content no longer matches the book's title.

For example, let's say that you came up with a great title for a book one day when you were out jogging. You were new to jogging, and you wanted to take the wealth of information you'd learned and turn it into a book. Suddenly, you come up with the perfect title: *I'll Jog to That.* Your original plan for your book was to inspire others to jog by encouraging them to jog for charities.

Titling Your Book

Initially, you'd planned to tell your readers to choose any charity, jog to bring awareness to that charity's cause, and post up your endeavors on your blog. But you've waited six months, and now that you're ready to start writing, you've gotten into other forms of fitness including weight training, kick boxing, and dance aerobics. Additionally, you're not just blogging about your endeavors anymore; nowadays, you're recording videos and writing articles for a local magazine. You want to incorporate everything that you're doing in your book now. As a matter of fact, you have some really good ideas, but you still like the title *I'll Jog to That*. Many authors today have this very same problem, and for this reason, it is never a good idea to entitle a book until you're finished writing it.

You may have a plan for your book, but one thing you'll learn as you write more books is that your plans will often be overridden by GOD'S plans. Sure, you likely have many

Titling Your Book

great ideas, but when writing a Christian book, you have to be prepared to let go of your "great" ideas to accept GOD'S plans for your book. Remember, it's not all about you; it's about the readers who will partake of the content of your book. GOD knows how to draw them with HIS WORD; whereas, your plan is to impress them with your words.

Coming up with a title for your book isn't as easy as it seems, and with some authors, it's actually harder to come up with a title than it is to write the content for a book. Of course, you should pray and ask GOD for a title. After all, GOD gave Adam permission to name the animals on earth. HE can and will give you permission to entitle your book. So, what if GOD leaves it up to you to name your book? How should you come up with the title? Below are seven pointers to consider when entitling your book.

1. **Consider the content.** Always remember that the title of the book

Titling Your Book

should represent the content of the book. What is your book about?

2. **Consider your target audience.** Every book has a target audience. Your target audience is the age group, race, marital status, gender, and socioeconomic status of the people who will most likely read your book.

When you locate your target audience, it'll be easier for you to draft up a title that will draw your audience. For example, let's say your book's audience turns out to be middle-class African American women ages 35-55. With your audience, you should not to use slang; you should be light on the wit, and you should never use stereotypical, judgmental speech.

3. **Find out what your target audience is interested in.** What types of movies would interest your target audience? What types of things do your target audience find offensive? Where does your target audience frequent? To find this out, you can search online for any

Titling Your Book

surveys that involve your target audience. You can also conduct surveys on your own. A good survey usually involves fifty to one hundred people. It's relatively easy to find people who are willing to fill out short surveys for nothing more than recognition in your book.

4. **Consider your way of talking.** Every one of us has a language, an accent, and a socioeconomic class. You have to understand that the way you speak and think may seem foreign to others, and people who can't relate to you will likely not buy your books. For this reason, you need to always write books that engage audiences who can understand and relate to you. Am I saying to limit yourself to that audience? Of course not. Get out and meet people from different socioeconomic classes so that you can relate to them, giving you the knowledge you'll need to write as

Titling Your Book

one of them. Know this: You can't write about a people unless you're one of them.

5. **Consider your goals.** Most authors want to write and sell best-selling books; books with a broader target audience, but there are some authors who only want to reach a certain demographic. It's up to you to determine who you want to reach, and be mindful of the audience you want to reach when writing and entitling your book.

6. **Consider yourself.** Can you handle success? Can you handle becoming a well-known, best-selling author with worldwide recognition? Some authors are truly afraid of the limelight. They want the money that comes with success, but they don't want the notoriety or the recognition that comes with success. What about you? If you want to draw a lot of new readers, you would have to come up with

Titling Your Book

controversial titles, but such titles draw many readers and much controversy. Can you handle opposition on a mass scale? If your answer is "yes," you can be as bold as you want to be, as long as you're prepared for the blessings and the backlash that comes with it.

7. **Consider your reach.** Let's face it, many people don't have large audiences that they can push their books to. Someone who is largely celebrated (celebrity) can entitle his or her book with whatever name he or she pleases without having to worry about losing book sales. But someone who doesn't have a large following won't have the luxury of entitling his or her book with just any name. That's why you should not entitle your book with boring titles that people can easily scroll by without noticing. Sometimes, controversial titles are good, and other times, they aren't such good ideas. It would depend on

Titling Your Book

whether or not those titles are deemed offensive.

Additionally, if you entitle your book with an offensive name, the content of that book had better be powerful enough to cool off your heated readers. People don't mind offensive titles if you're able to explain away the title and empower them at the same time. You have to determine what title is right for your book, and whether or not you are able to endure the blessings or the backlash that comes with a controversial title.

8. **Consider your book's depth.** Some books are thought-provoking and revelation-bearing, and such books need titles that speak to the depth of the book. Books that reach even the most analytical and critical of souls can have what we consider some of the most controversial titles, or even titles that don't make sense.

    Take the book, *Pigs in a Parlor*, for example. I've heard that the book is

Titling Your Book

extremely popular; therefore, the authors could title their book *Pigs in a Parlor* and not worry about losing sales. Instead, the title is so unique that it only inspires more sales from curious souls who want to know what pigs in a parlor have to do with demonic entities. At the same time, one of the reviews I read under the book was a one star review from a woman who thought the book was about swine farming. It's safe to say that if you want to create a title that's strange, you'd better have content that makes up for the appeal lost in the title.

When coming up with a title for your book, always think objectively. What if you were out somewhere and you saw a book with the title you're considering? Would you buy that book, or would you flip through the pages, and then put it back on the shelf? Are you sold out on the ideas that you're presenting in that book, or

Titling Your Book

is your mind subject to change?

The best way to title a book (outside of hearing from GOD) is to:

1. Determine what the book is about.
2. List five to ten words that describe the book's subject matter.
3. Determine which of those words are popularly used.
4. Play around with the words to see if you can come up with a creative title that explains the book's content, all the while, inspiring people to want to buy your book.
5. Conduct a Google search, and search Amazon for any books with that same title. It is always better to come up with an original title than it is to come out with what others may perceive as a copy-cat title.
6. If someone else has a book with that title, consider adjusting your title a little so that your title will be unique to you.

Titling Your Book

For example, if you had chosen to name your book *Rose Petals on Fire*, and you discovered that someone else had given their book that same name, the best remedy is to readjust your book's name. You could revise the name and entitle your book *Rose Petals on a Fire*, *Fiery Rose Petals*, or *Rose Petal Inferno*. You may find that in trying the name with other words synonymous with one of the words in your previously chosen title, you may come up with a better name.

7. Use a thesaurus and play around with the words you've decided that were synonymous with your book's subject matter. The goal isn't to choose the first name that jumps out at you. It's to develop multiple titles to consider, and then ask a few non-aspiring authors which name they'd go with, or which title they'd buy. The reason I said non-aspiring authors is because people who write or aspire to write can easily see

Titling Your Book

your title as a goldmine, steal it, and publish a book under that title.

The best way to locate your target audience is to write a series of blog posts, and gather up about one hundred people to read your posts. You can do this online simply by asking people on social networks if they'll read your posts and fill out a short survey. Create a survey asking your readers what they thought of the posts, which age group they thought the posts were better suited for, and ask them if they would consider buying your books. Ask them to be straightforward and share their honest feedback. You can even give them the ability to answer your questions anonymously if they aren't comfortable placing their names on the answers.

Make sure these people are not personally involved in your life, otherwise, they may be too afraid to be truthful with you, or they may allow their personal feelings about you influence their answers. Additionally, make

Titling Your Book

sure the survey gathers their age, race, economic status, and religious denomination. This way, you'll locate your target audience and you'll discover which demographic is most likely to purchase your books. When you know who's most likely to purchase and read your books, you'll know who you're writing for.

Always remember to identify your target audience, and don't get too fancy with the title. All too often, new authors become so fascinated with words that they choose words that the average person does not understand. In other words, don't pick up a thesaurus trying to find a word synonymous with "experience" and come out with "perspicacity". Sure, you may be excited once you discover what "perspicacity" means, but your potential readers will not buy a book if they've got to purchase a dictionary along with that book. Remember, readers like to flow, and if the title of your book tells a person that they'll need extra help reading it, they likely won't buy your

Titling Your Book

book. It's not about sounding or appearing intelligent; it's about educating and entertaining your readers. If you do that, you've got a potential best-seller on your hands.

Characters & Character Dialogues

Choosing characters for your book can be easy if you're really sociable, but if you're reclusive and don't know too many people outside of the ones you've grown up with, choosing characters may be an arduous task. In other words, if you're shy and antisocial, you probably don't know enough people to display a range of personalities in your writings. For this reason, it is always good for writers to speak and get to know people who are unlike themselves and the people they normally hang around.

As an editor and publisher, I've read my fair share of fictional books, and one thing I've noticed with a lot of authors who attempt to write fiction is their inability to display varying

Characters & Character Dialogues

personalities in their characters. All of their characters speak in the same manner, and if there was no name to identify who said what, the readers would be at a loss. When writing a fictional book, your readers should be able to identify a character based on something he or she said.

For example, let's say that you have six characters in your book. The main character is Shelly, and the other characters are Pete, Bob, Bruce, Karen, and Stephanie. Every one of these characters should have a personality that identifies them, and forewarns the reader about something they have done or may potentially do.

Let's say that Shelly (the main character) is shy and secretive. Pete is in love with Shelly, and he's very protective of her and everyone in the group. Bob is the comedian of the group, and he's always pulling stunts to make his friends laugh. Bruce is an insensitive jerk who absolutely has no tact. Bruce's character is obviously a wounded soul who loves to offend

Characters & Character Dialogues

others, but Bruce is also defensive of his friends, thus the reason they keep him around. Karen has a crush on Pete, but Pete's in love with Shelly. Karen is jealous-hearted, insecure and promiscuous. Stephanie is the level-headed Christian in the group who seems to see everything, and is always trying to get her friends to come to church with her. This would be your rough-draft of each person, and it would help you to determine what type of personality you want to attach to each character.

In this skit, let's say Shelly receives an anonymous email from someone claiming Pete had been badmouthing Shelly at a party. Who would you believe that this email came from? Karen, of course! Karen has a crush on Pete, and Karen is a jealous soul; therefore, you'd know that the personality you should attach to Karen would include negative thinking, negative speaking, flirtatious, conniving, and intelligent. You wouldn't want to make Karen

Characters & Character Dialogues

too obvious; you'd want your readers to believe that they'd figured something out about Karen that others obviously can't see. People don't like stories that pretty much lay out the details for them; they like to think that they figured it out themselves.

When choosing characters for your book, you should always have different personality types. This would increase your target audience, and at the same time, it would keep the book interesting. Some of your readers will read the entire book looking for conversations between Pete and Shelly. They may be fascinated by the other characters, but people often find one or two characters that they like the most, and they'll read an entire book just to see what happens with those characters.

When giving your characters personalities and names, always consider the demographic of those characters. For example, if your book's characters are upper-class Asian-Americans,

Characters & Character Dialogues

you would need to know how upper-class Asian-Americans usually speak, as well as how they reason. If your book was about lower-class Asian-Americans, you would need to know how lower-class Asian-Americans speak, as well as how they reason. This means that you would have to hang out in communities where your demographic lives, or you'd have to frequent places that are frequented by your demographic. At the same time, you wouldn't name an Asian-American woman Becky or Keisha. You would want to go with a more traditional Asian name, or you could go with a common American name like Jenny or Ann. The easiest way to come up with names for your characters is by conducting a search via a search engine such as Google. For example, if you were looking for Asian-American female names, you would Google, "Asian American female names." You'll find a list of websites that have Asian-American female names listed on them, and you could choose any of those names. Additionally, always go with names

Characters & Character Dialogues

that your readers can pronounce. For difficult names, be sure to list the name's pronunciation (example: Kameni/ Pronounced Kuh-men-ee). You can also create an index at the beginning of the book listing the names of the characters, who they are, and the pronunciation of their names.

When choosing characters, it always helps if you know people who have some of the traits you're instilling in your characters. For example, if your book takes place at a school, and you listed Frederick as the class clown, it would be good if you'd known a few class clowns in your day. You could take pieces of their personalities and create Frederick with a personality to call his own.

Character dialogue should be unpredictable and engaging. Dialogue should always display the varying personalities of each individual character. Check out the poor dialogue below.

Characters & Character Dialogues

Mariah: Jason, I'm tired.

Jason: Why are you tired, Mariah?

Mariah: You don't treat me right anymore.

Jason: What do you mean I don't treat you right? Mariah, I love you.

Mariah: Jason, I'm leaving you because you don't treat me right and you don't like to listen.

Jason: Please don't leave me, Mariah. I'll change.

Mariah: No, Jason; it's too late. I'm tired and I want to go to sleep. Please do not call my house anymore, Jason.

Jason: Before you hang up, please know that I love you, Mariah.

Mariah: Okay, Jason. I am hanging up the phone now.

It would appear there is absolutely no help for this dialogue or the author. That's because this dialogue reads as if it were written by a child. What human beings on the face of this earth constantly say the same things, while repeating each others' names while saying it? Dialogue

Characters & Character Dialogues

must sound natural and unscripted. When reading this dialogue, you'll likely envision two actors who are in dire need of acting classes on the screen of a low-budget movie. Let's revise the dialogue to make it sound a little more professional.

Mariah: Jason, I'm tired.

Jason: What do you mean you're tired? What have I done this time?

Mariah: That's just it! You haven't done a thing! You're constantly wanting me to be little Ms. Perfect for you and your mother! You ignore me half of the time, and when you are paying attention to me, it's only because you want something from me. You don't treat me right and I can't take it anymore!

Jason: What do you mean I don't treat you right? Mariah, I love you, but I cannot take all of this bickering. You could have resolved whatever problems you had with my mother a long time ago, but you chose to be stubborn! I don't know what's worse: You blaming me for

Characters & Character Dialogues

the breakdown of our relationship or to hear you say you're leaving me because of my mother! That's pathetic, Mariah...really pathetic!

Mariah: Listen to you! You're so full of yourself that you can't see a good thing when it's staring you right in your face! I'm not leaving you because of your mother; I'm leaving you because of how you allow your mother to treat me! I'm leaving you because you don't treat me right and you don't like to listen to anything I say! Like, on Saturday, I tried to talk to you about some problems I was having at work, and you totally ignored me! Can you imagine how I felt? I needed you and you weren't there for me! You're never there!

Jason: Wait. Let's just calm down and talk about this rationally. I love you and you love me, and that's all that matters. Every couple has problems, and we're no different.

Mariah: Yeah, well...I don't want our problems anymore, so it's over Jason. It's over.

Jason: Let's just talk about this. Please, let's

85

Characters & Character Dialogues

sit down without all of the emotions and talk this thing out. I'm willing to change if you are.

Mariah: No, Jason; it's too late. Don't you understand? I'm tired. I just can't take this relationship and all that it comes with anymore. I'm sorry, but it's over.

Jason: Well, have things your way! I tried to reason with you, but I forgot, I'm always the bad guy! I'm always the one who's doing wrong! I asked to talk about the problem, and you're still saying that it's over! I don't care, Mariah! I love you, but if it's over...it's just over! Have a good life!

----*End of example.*

With this dialogue, we can conclude that Mariah is emotional and she's fed up with Jason. No amount of words is going to change her mind. We can also conclude that Jason is really determined to keep Mariah, but when Jason doesn't get his way, Jason can be a hot-head. So, we got a chance to see a little of Mariah and Jason's personalities. It would be

Characters & Character Dialogues

easy to put Jason in a follow-up conversation
with a friend of his based on his personality.
Since we know that Jason loves Mariah, we
can conclude that Jason is going to be
somewhat emotional and angry about the
breakup. He's likely not going to let go easily,
but anytime he's rejected, we know that Jason
may react strongly before calming down and
attempting to resolve the matter. Let's place
Jason in a conversation with his brother,
Jonathan.

Jonathan: Hey. What's going on, Jason?
You've been kinda grumpy all day. Is
something wrong?

Jason: Mariah and I broke up, but it's okay. I
did everything right by that girl, but I just can't
make her happy. I guess what ticks me off the
most is that she keeps saying that I let Mom
get in the way of our relationship. Maybe Mom
was right. Maybe Mariah is too trashy to be in
a relationship with anyone with aspirations.

Jonathan: Jason, I'm just gonna tell you this
once, but don't say anything to Mom. I don't

Characters & Character Dialogues

want to hurt her feelings. Mom can be a little too judgmental, and I think that's because she doesn't have anyone in her life right now. Do you remember when I was dating Amy from up the street?

Jason: Yeah.

Jonathan: Well, Mom said Amy wasn't fit to marry a dog. At first, I thought that Mom was perfect, so I asked her why she didn't like Amy. Do you know what she told me? She said that Amy dyed her hair and she was always wearing her sister's hand-me-downs. She said that Amy would end up with five kids by five different men, living in a trailer home and drinking her life away. I trusted Mom, so I broke up with Amy. It's been about five years since Amy and I broke up, and since then, Amy has went to college and is now in medical school, and she's engaged to Doctor Frank Olsterwitz from Olsterwitz Medical.

To this day, I've regretted breaking up with that girl. She was a really good girl, but I stayed away from her because that's what made Mom

Characters & Character Dialogues

happy. By the time I figured out how Mom was, I tried to reconcile with Amy, but it was too late. She was dating Dr. Frank.

Jason: So, you're saying that I shouldn't have let Mom get involved in my relationship with Mariah?

Jonathan: Bingo! That's exactly what I'm saying. I think Mom means well, but her heart is just in the wrong place. If it were left up to her, we'd never marry or move out of her house. I think she's just lonely. I'm gonna be marrying Nicole in three months, and I wouldn't be meeting my dream girl at the altar if I'd listened to Mom or if I'd let her interfered with my relationship.

Jason: I guess I just wanted to make Mom happy, but it's almost impossible to make both Mom and Mariah happy.

Jonathan: Of course it is. Mom didn't like Nicole, and she did everything in her power to turn me against Nicole, but do you know what I told her? I told her that if she couldn't accept Nicole, she'd lose me too. You see, with Mom,

Characters & Character Dialogues

you've got to put your foot down, otherwise, she'll ruin every relationship you get in, and she'll find something wrong with every girl you get with. That's just how she is. Like I said, she's lonely.

Jason: Okay, so what should I do now? Mariah wants nothing to do with me.

Jonathan: Talk to Mariah. Matter of fact, go and get her some roses. Tell her that you love her and that you won't be letting Mom get in you guys' way anymore.

Mariah's a good girl. Try not to loose your cool with her, Jason. She seems to be a little high strung and emotional. Be gentle with her. Just talk to her and tell her how you feel. If that doesn't work, just let it go, and the next time you get in a relationship, don't let Mom interfere.

----*End of example.*

You'll notice that Jason's personality is becoming more and more familiar to you. We still see that he is hurt and he wants to work

Characters & Character Dialogues

things out with Mariah. We can also conclude that Jonathan is Jason's older brother. So, in giving a personality to Jonathan, we'd give him a personality that's typical of older, more mature brothers.

When writing dialogues, always think and speak as the character whose dialogue you're writing. For example, if you're writing as Jason, put yourself in Jason's shoes. You wouldn't turn Jason into a tattoo-covered, manic-depressive soul who frequented bars. Jason's character reads like a somewhat young man, maybe around eighteen to twenty-one years old. He sounds somewhat inexperienced with life, because we can see that he's given his mother too much power, he doesn't have a handle on his emotions, and he's a little lost in how he should deal with Mariah. Additionally, we can conclude that Jonathan has taken on the fatherly role around the house, and Jonathan has learned to assert himself with his mother when needed. At the

Characters & Character Dialogues

same time, Jonathan is careful not to hurt his mother's feelings, so even though he's asserted himself with her, he doesn't want to offend his mother. So, in a character dialogue between Jonathan and his mother, we'd portray Jonathan as respectful of his mother, but not afraid to tell her when she's wrong.

In the movies, you'll notice an array of personalities that are typical to some of the people you've met in your life. Being able to relate to or recognize character types is what makes a movie great to most of us. Let's take Tyler Perry's Madea character, for example. Being an African American woman from the south (Mississippi), I recognized the Madea character, and that's what made the character so funny. I've had two Madeas in my family, and they were both strict and persistent. They were also very protective of their families, and they were women who liked to host large gatherings just to cook.
Many African Americans like myself can relate

Characters & Character Dialogues

to the Madea character, so it was not surprising that Madea would become such a big hit. Needless to say, many authors who attempt to write fiction could not develop a character that would garner nationwide recognition because their characters all sound the same; they simply have no personalities assigned to them.

Get out and meet the character types you intend to portray. If some of those character types are dangerous, don't go out and meet them; instead, try to study their behaviors from a distance. You can watch movies that portray your character types, or you can read articles that demonstrate the mindset of the character types you want to portray. Additionally, there are tons of resources online to read or view. Just utilize the search engine of your choice, and always remember that good writing often requires a lot of research. You can't rush a book worth reading.

Book Fluffing

Ordinarily, I could simply list "book fluffing" as one of the things that you should avoid. It would be nothing more than just another pointer on a list of things an author shouldn't do, but I wanted to dedicate an entire chapter to this to help you understand the difference between good fluffing and bad fluffing.

What is book fluffing? Book fluffing is the attempt of an author to make their book's thicker without adding more text or by adding a bunch of useless text. This is more commonly done with authors who intend to have their books available in print than it is with e-book authors. The most common ways to fluff a book is:

- Adding images to a book.
- Adding 1.5 line spacing or double

Book Fluffing

spacing the lines in a book.

- Adding a bunch of quotes and long scriptures to a book.
- Adding a bunch of useless text to a book.

The truth is, most authors fluff their books. You can go to Amazon, and purchase a twenty-five page e-book, only to find that the author used double-spaced lines, a lot of scriptures and added an extensive opening to the book (example: foreword, introduction, preface, acknowledgments, dedications, and so on). In such a book, you may find that the author wrote a total of ten actual pages, but the other fifteen pages are nothing but fluff. Of course, this infuriates buyers because they've paid their money to get a book, only to receive a well-dressed article or blog post.

When I launched *Anointed Fire Magazine*, I advertised to get writers for the magazine. I received a lot of applications, and at first, I

Book Fluffing

accepted almost everyone who applied. If they were Christian and they wanted to write, they were approved. I told the writers that they were to write articles that were at least five hundred words in length. Every month, I would receive articles from the writers, and every month I would see the differences between the writers.

Some writers would send in articles of exactly five hundred words or just a little over five hundred words, but it was clear to me that they did not like to write. Their articles were oftentimes late, and I would have to email them repeatedly asking for the material. Then, there were the passionate writers. Their articles would be two thousand words or more, and their articles were always early. The passionate writers had more depth to their articles, and it was obvious that they'd put time into researching for their articles. Some of the more passionate writers would even ask me if they could send in more than one article a month. Additionally, the passionate writers

Book Fluffing

stuck around more; whereas, the not-so-passionate writers would quit because having to submit an article (albeit short) once a month was just too much for them. The point is: Passionate writers take the time to write, research, and review their books. Passionate writers are gifted by GOD to write. It's not a struggle for them, but for a person who has to squeeze a few words out, writing may not be what they're gifted to do.

I could ask a passionate writer to write a five thousand word article about Christian marriage and why it's under attack, and I'd have that article back in less than a week. I could ask a not-so-passionate writer to write me a five hundred word article about the same subject, and if I don't give that writer a deadline, it would be months before I would receive a completed, non-researched article. Additionally, I would have to beg, remind, and maybe even offer some sort of incentive to the writer who's not gifted to write because writing,

Book Fluffing

for him or her, is like pulling teeth from a lion. A person who's not gifted to write is more likely to add bad fluff to their books than a person who is gifted to write.

What's the difference between good fluff and bad fluff? Good fluff is simply thickening up your book with a line spacing of no more than 1.5. Fluffing is only good when the author has written a good, well-written book that they simply want to make a little thicker. For example, if you wrote a book that was fifty pages in length, but you wanted that book to be thicker so you could have a spine on it, it's okay to fluff the book. Just don't over-fluff it. Bad fluffing is when an author has more spaces in their book than they have text. The worst form of fluffing is when an author adds a bunch of useless text, stories, and dialogues to their books in an attempt to make their books thicker. For example, let's say an author writes a book about a woman who'd just learned that her now twelve-year-old daughter was

Book Fluffing

switched at birth by the hospital's staff.
Victoria goes on a mission to locate her
biological daughter, and while she's looking for
her daughter, the hospital does everything in
their power to keep Victoria from finding out the
truth. They even have her arrested for
trespassing, citing that they'd banned her from
the premises after she'd called and threatened
a nurse.

The author rushes through what should have
been at least a hundred page book, and she
sums it up to thirty pages. Realizing that her
book would have no spine, the author decides
to fluff her book. She double-spaces her book
and adds a scene where Victoria is on the
telephone with her husband. Her husband is
stationed in Afghanistan, and is trying to get
home to help his wife find their daughter. The
conversation is lengthy, and to sum it up, it's
basically Victoria and her husband talking
about what she's done so far.

The readers know what she's done, so
reintroducing this information in the form of

Book Fluffing

conversation is pointless. The conversation is only good if the conversation brings about new revelation or if Victoria's husband encourages her to fight for their daughter. Needless to say, you should never reintroduce.

Another way authors add useless text to their books is by using a method I refer to as "circling the drain." That's when an author does not get to the point, but instead, takes up too much of the readers' time saying the same things repeatedly, only using different words. This form of fluffing indicates that the author isn't creative or the author does not want to put anymore thought into the book. You see, as you write, you'll come to understand that every new piece of information you insert in the book has to be explained. Once some authors realize that they have to put more time into their stories every time they introduce new information, they stop reintroducing new info, and they start repeating what they'd previously written. An example of "circling the drain"

Book Fluffing

would be:

Tony covered his mouth with his hand. He couldn't believe what he was seeing. Tony blinked his eyes because he wanted to make sure that he wasn't dreaming. He couldn't believe his eyes, so Tony pinched himself. Could this be real? After he pinched himself, Tony realized that he wasn't dreaming. He was really seeing his wife in the car with his best friend, and they were kissing. Why would Samantha be in the car kissing Michael? The adulterous duo were in the car kissing right in front of Tony and Samantha's house. Why would Samantha betray her husband? ----*End of example.*

As you can see, we're using a lot of words, but we aren't going anywhere. We get it: Tony saw his wife kissing his best friend, but what next? Your readers will want to see the story unfolding; they won't want to sit for five minutes reading about how Tony is standing on the curb crying while his wife is in the car kissing his

Book Fluffing

best friend. Your readers will not want to spend two minutes waiting for Tony to realize that he's not dreaming. Your readers will not want to spend several minutes waiting on you to finish repeating the same questions over and over again as if they can answer them. Sure, you want to speak as Tony and ask the questions that Tony is inwardly asking himself, but at the same time, you need to leave the line of questioning and get to the point. Don't keep asking the same questions repeatedly.

Another form of good or acceptable fluffing is adding images to your book, but always remember that the images must relate to the book's content. Additionally, if you're writing a book for adults, take it easy on the images. Most adults buy books for the text and would prefer not to see images, unless it's a self-help book, and the images serve as instructional tools.

Finally, it's good (and highly recommended)

Book Fluffing

that with a Christian book, you copy and paste scriptures from an online Bible. What's not recommended, however, is that you have more pasted text (scriptures or quotes) in your book than actual text. It goes without saying that you shouldn't have an even amount of actual text as you have pasted text. Pasted text should make up twenty percent of your book or less. Pasted text should be there to compliment or add to your book; it should never become the book itself.

When you decided to write a book, you took on a responsibility to entertain, educate, and inform your readers. Always remember to take your book seriously, and don't spend too much time trying to avoid doing the work of actually writing a book. Instead, use your time to improve your book. Bad authors always get bad reviews, and one bad review can cost you hundreds, and sometimes thousands of sales. Your readers will spend their money to get your books, and they will spend their time reading

Book Fluffing

your books. Make sure it's time and money
well spent.

25 Rules to Write By

1. Each character should have his or her own personality. For example, if you're portraying Canton as an animated, but loving man, it would be good to mention how his energy made others feel. Anytime you speak of Canton, his personality should show, and if Canton is to get sick, you'd show how his personality had been affected by his illness.

2. Each character should have his or her own way of speaking. Remember, you don't sound like your friends or family members. You all have your own speaking voices, word choices and ways of driving home a point. Your way of speaking is your vocal personality. Don't give your characters the same

25 Rules to Write By

vocal personalities, otherwise, your readers will be angry that they've paid good money for a bad read.

3. Conversations should be listed in narrative or dialogue format. The proper way to write dialogue is in narrative format, but some writers prefer script format. For example, review the conversation below:

Narrative Format

Preston looked at his mother with hurt in his eyes.

"Take me to my Dad's house," said Preston. "You keep saying that you're going to let me visit my Dad, but you never do! Take me to my Dad's house now!"

Donna was hurt and confused. Why had Preston suddenly started showing interest in his father?

"I'm not taking you to that man's house!" exclaimed Donna.

25 Rules to Write By

"Why?"

"Because, he's a monster! If your Dad hadn't left me, we wouldn't have to move out of our house right now! Don't you get it?! We can't afford that house because your Dad left!"

Preston's little face turned red as he listened to his mother badgering his father yet again.
"I don't care. Your problems with Dad are your problems with Dad, not mine!"

Dialogue (Script) Format
Preston: Take me to my Dad's house. You keep saying that you're going to let me visit my Dad, but you never do! Take me to my Dad's house now!
Donna: I'm not taking you to that man's house!
Preston: Why?
Donna: Because, he's a monster! If your Dad hadn't left me, we wouldn't have to move out of our house right now! Don't you get it?! We can't afford that house because your Dad left!

25 Rules to Write By

Preston: I don't care. Your problems with Dad are your problems with Dad, not mine!

----*End of example.*

The most popular and more traditional form of listing dialogue is in narrative format. With narrative format, each speaker gets his or her own paragraph when speaking. Script format is most commonly used for playwriting, but it's slowly making its way as a popular format in short stories and novels.

4. Every character introduced by name should have a role in the book. Introducing characters one time is confusing to a reader who's expecting to see more of that character. I've read many books where the author has introduced characters, and after the character's introduction, the character was never heard or seen again. Think of movie scripts. Movie producers will

25 Rules to Write By

always try to find ways to cut costs
when producing a movie; therefore, they
won't use characters who spring up and
disappear. If they do, the character will
have a role in which they cause the
main actor or the villain to rethink their
policies or positions. For example, a
good extra would be a pawn shop
owner. Let's say that the main character
has been looking for a ring that was
stolen from a little old lady. The old lady
is a widow, and the ring was precious to
her because it was the only token of her
husband's love that she had left. The
main character is going from pawn shop
to pawn shop trying to find that ring.
Suddenly, he walks into a pawn shop
where the owner tells him that the ring
isn't there, but gives him valuable
information as to how he could locate
the ring. He's considered a valuable
extra because he adds something to the
script.

25 Rules to Write By

5. Many authors throw characters into their books just for the sake of using a name that they like. Maybe they promised little Julio that they'd use his name in the book. So, they add a Julio, and his only role is to walk up to the main character and ask for directions. After that, Julio is never heard from again. What was the point of having Julio ask for directions if Julio's character isn't adding anything to the book? The only time that it would be a great idea to add Julio is if Julio's question sparked a revelation in the main character's mind. That's when Julio would be a valuable extra. Nevertheless, because Julio didn't have any other roles in the book, it's not important or advisable that we know his name. Instead, we would refer to him as "the man who asked for directions."

6. Every character that has a role should be given a conclusion. For example, let's say you're writing a story about a

112

25 Rules to Write By

girl named Felicia. Felicia has a little sister who's always getting in trouble. In the beginning of the book, you say that Felicia's little sister has been arrested and Felicia had to bail her out. Later on in the book, you slowly get away from Felicia's little sister and the other characters' stories take on lives of their own. Your readers will want to know what happened to Felicia's little sister. Just dropping her from the story is a huge mistake. She doesn't have to have a major role, but readers should be updated about her.

7. If you introduce a situation, always give a conclusion or end to that situation. Let's go back to the example of Felicia's little sister again.

If you're saying she's a troublemaker, you need to go on to say what happened to her as a result of her troublemaking. Leaving unanswered questions does not set you up for part two of your book; it sets you up for a

25 Rules to Write By

bunch of disgruntled readers who will be anxious to leave you poor reviews.

8. Every scene or situation should be detailed. Taking readers to a place and dropping them off somewhere else will only confuse and upset them. For example, let's say that Terrence is in the witness protection program, and he's running from a drug ring that he was once a part of. Review the short story below to see how poorly it's written.

Terrence was paranoid because a drug lord had told him that he was going to kill him and his family. Terrence was scared, and the police had placed him and his family in witness protection. They were living in a cabin outside of Utah, and the cabin was old. The floors creaked, the bed had bedbugs and the cabin stunk. Terrence and his wife decided to call the district attorney that following Monday to tell him about their living conditions.

----End of example.

How can we conclude that this story is poorly

25 Rules to Write By

written? It's simple. It would appear that the author is trying to rush through details without actually causing the reader to experience what the characters are experiencing. This is lazy writing at its best. Let's review a better way to write the story.

Terrence was paranoid. Chainsaw, the drug lord, had previously promised Terrence that he'd not only find him and his family, but that he'd take his time killing them. Terrence was haunted by the memories of having watched two of his closest friends be slaughtered by the same monster that was seeking to take his life.

The sound of the creeping house always made Terrence nervous. Why would the police hide him in such an old house? It seemed as if they wanted to make his stay in witness protection as agonizing as possible. Even the bed was loud. Anytime Terrence and his wife, Pam, would lie down at night, the bed would sound as if it were screaming their location to the world.

25 Rules to Write By

The air wreaked of rotten wood, and the broken toilet in the bathroom made living in the cabin even more unbearable. The stench of feces mixed with the smell of rotten wood, creating a putrid smell that made the couple nauseous. To make matters worse, Terrence and Pam's bed was full of bed bugs. The pillows smelled as if they hadn't been washed in centuries, and the comforter had unidentifiable stains all over it.

Terrence was disgusted and Pam was losing her mind. The couple sat down and discussed their living arrangements. They were fed up with the poor treatment they'd been receiving from the state police department. Surely, the state could afford to give them better accommodations, so they made up their minds to call the district attorney that following Monday to tell him about their living arrangements.

----*End of example.*

One thing you'll likely notice is your facial

25 Rules to Write By

expressions as you read about Terrence and Pam's living conditions. Your facial expressions likely changed as you read about the smell in the home, the bed bugs and the dirty comforter. Either way, you experienced what the characters were experiencing, so you're now passionate about seeing the characters be placed in better conditions. If I rushed you through the story, however, you wouldn't have too much time to think, react or feel for the characters. You'd just see a bunch of words describing a situation in the same way a police officer writes a police report: Short and to the point.

9. Make sure every problematic or traumatic situation teaches a lesson. Nothing ticks a reader off more than having been dragged into a traumatic situation, only to have the author give a swift end to that situation with no explanation or lesson. For example, if you say Felicia was raped, you would then be responsible for going after

25 Rules to Write By

Felicia's rapist with your pen. Readers will want to know what happened to the rapist, and what was the reason for having Felicia get raped. Just writing about her being raped will upset many readers, but just as you've angered them with the rape scene, you have to cool them off and give them what they want: justice and an explanation.

10. Every fictional story should have heroes, just as every fictional story should have villains. As a Christian writer, you should know that GOD is always the hero, and any human heroic character should gather his or her strength from the LORD, and they should give glory to the LORD. Glorifying GOD is the heart of all Christian writing. A book that glorifies man is secular, even if it has CHRIST as its undertones.

11. Never let the villain win in the end. People hate to see the villain get ahead, and will oftentimes close books

25 Rules to Write By

whenever the villain is getting the best of the good guy. It's normal that the villain will get the best of the good guy at some point, but it's also expected for the good guy to get the training he needs to overcome evil in the end. If your villain wins, your book glorifies evil.

12. Never let the hero die in the end. You'll upset your readers. Sure, we've seen stories where the hero dies, and we've all cried at the sight of his passing. At the same time, we've seen good movies be ruined by the useless killing of a hero or a character, and this causes movies to get lower ratings from viewers. You want to teach, inspire and excite your readers. It is never good to depress the readers for absolutely no reason. I've read plenty of fictional books where people die senselessly, and their deaths don't add to the book, don't inspire the main character to win, and only seem to upset and confuse the readers. The

25 Rules to Write By

hero is not supposed to die, in a reader's view. It's okay to kill him or her off, but always remember, it is better to keep the hero alive or raise up a new hero than to just kill someone with your pen and give no justifiable explanation for your actions.

13. Don't just kill off the book's characters for no reason. One of the worst mistakes some Christian authors make is bringing characters into their stories only to kill them off. Remember, you are the orchestrator of the events carried out in your book. If people are just dying for no reason, or they're dying just to give the main character a dramatic scene, you've missed the whole idea behind Christian writing. For example, let's say that Marcia is the main character in your book, and Marcia has a best friend named Debra. Marcia's obstacle is her dance teacher. Marcia wants to dance professionally, but her

25 Rules to Write By

dance teacher gets the final say in who's placed in the televised Grand Dance Off. Debra's been encouraging Marcia, but suddenly, Debra has a seizure and dies. Now, Marcia's mad and even more encouraged to win. This would sound like a Hollywood plot, but in truth, even Hollywood knows better. If Debra dies, she has to die because of something related to the dance or the dance competition. To make it read better, we'd say that Debra was also a dancer, and even though she'd told the teacher about her heart condition, the teacher was merciless and wouldn't let Debra take the breaks she needed. Now, we can justify Marcia's anger and her desire to take the dancing teacher down. But just killing off Debra to tick off Marcia is pointless.

14. Never give the hero a swift victory. Readers need to see the struggle of the hero in his or her attempt to defeat

whatever foe you introduce. Swift victory equates to a lazy author, in a reader's eyes. Think about real life. Most of the trials and tribulations that you've endured were somewhat lengthy, and your victory wasn't instantaneous. Instead, you had to endure, and at some point, it looked as if the enemy would take the victory. Nevertheless, you prevailed (through CHRIST) in the end. Your stories should read the same way real life plays out.

15. Any character that dies should have a personality, and that person's story should be told. For example, let's say that your main character's name is Douglas. The story is about the struggles Douglas faced as he attempted to achieve his life-long goal of becoming a professional football player. Suddenly, you decide to kill off Douglas's mother, and the readers are taken through scenes of Douglas crying,

25 Rules to Write By

being ministered to, and almost giving up on his dream. People need to know who Douglas's mother was, how she inspired him, and how he supported her throughout her sickness (if she was sick) or how she came to have an accident (if that was your method of killing her off). Just saying that he got a call that she was dead, and then, having him suddenly show up at her funeral is bad writing. Remember, you can't write books the same way movies cast scenes.

In a movie, Douglas may receive a call, and then, suddenly, the viewers are at the funeral watching Douglas break down as his mother is lowered into the grave, but in a book, the readers need more details. If someone decides to make a movie of your book, they will remove the added details.

16. Every story should have a problem and a resolution. Just taking people for a mental stroll with no bumps in the road

25 Rules to Write By

is the quickest way to bore them to sleep. A good book lists a challenge, a person or a group of people affected by that challenge, and a person (hero) who overcomes that challenge.

17. Remember, your readers are emotional creatures who will want to experience joy. Don't write long, depressing stories with good endings. You've depressed your readers, and a good ending won't compensate for that.

Instead, list the challenge, show the main character's efforts and failures to overcome that challenge, and then, show victory. Also, show some great points in the book that make the readers smile, laugh, and scream the characters' names.

Fictional books aren't for everyone. If you aren't good with character roles, personalities and scenes, please stick with non fiction books. It's okay if you aren't a great fictional writer; that's probably not the area of writing that GOD has called you to. If your stories are

25 Rules to Write By

rushed, and you're not patient, then you should consider other genres of writing.

18. Never ever change the main character. The main character is who your readers have gotten to know; it is who they now relate themselves to. One of the silliest things you can do is have one main character, and suddenly, create another main character. The only time that it's okay to change the main character is when someone else is taking the main character's place in an attempt to rescue the main character, or if your book tells several stories with several main characters.

Let's say that Pastor Alex is in jail because he'd protested an abortion clinic. Your readers will want the good pastor released, so it's okay to have Pastor Alex's best friend, Randy temporarily take on the main character role. That's because we are now seeing Randy work at getting Pastor Alex released. We will also need to see Pastor Alex's living conditions,

25 Rules to Write By

experience his frustration, and witness some of what happens to him while he's waiting to be released.

19. Never put characters into fights or disagreements without telling the readers the purpose of those battles, and why there was a need to insert those battles. All too often, writers see the need to insert some type of drama into their scenes, so they pencil in unnecessary and unexplained fights and confrontations.

Every fight your characters enter must be associated with the main plot of the book. Saying that Andy slapped Arnold, and then offering no information as to what led Andy to strike Arnold is error. Your readers need to know why Andy struck Arnold and how it ties in with your book's plot.

20. Never make the main character a villain; otherwise, your readers will not want to relate to him or her, and will not read your entire book. Always remember,

126

25 Rules to Write By

your readers will see themselves as the main character. If they can't relate to or do not want to relate to the main character, they won't finish your book.

21. Never give detailed sex scenes in any Christian book. Talk about what led up to the occurrence of sex, but never give the details of sex; otherwise, you will be guilty of engaging in soft (mental) porn. Remember this: Your readers should not be aroused reading your book.

22. Do not scene jump. It's not a movie; it's a book. Keep the readers in one place until you explain them out of it. The pencil is in your hand, and the keyboard is under your fingertips; therefore, you have the power to create a place that all of your readers will visit.

You can't put them into time machines or toss them from one scene to the other. If you're talking about Alisha having trouble with a problematic customer and she's about to call the police on that customer, keep the readers

25 Rules to Write By

at the scene. Don't take them over to Linda's house where Linda and her husband are having a disagreement. You'll only confuse and infuriate your readers. Remember, you're writing a book, not a movie script. You can, however, add scene breaks and change the scenes.

23. Always pay attention to the character names, and make sure you don't get one character confused with the other. I have yet to see a fictional book (before editing) where one or more of the characters weren't called by another character's name or given an entirely different name altogether.

The issue is: We take breaks when writing. We write a little on Monday, and we come back to write a little more on Wednesday. By Wednesday, we may have forgotten some of our character's names, and we may end up calling a character Jason in one part of our books, only to start calling him Jacob later on. The best way to remedy this is to take a

25 Rules to Write By

separate piece of paper and write down every character's name as you input them in the story. Once you're done, conduct a search for each character's name to see how you used it. You can conduct a search by simultaneously pressing Ctrl + F on your keyboard. This will open a box on your computer. Type the characters' names in the box one by one, and go back and reread how you used their names. Also, have a few trusted friends reread your book. Again, I have never seen a fictional book (before editing) where the characters hadn't been accidentally switched.

24. Don't make your characters, character dialogues, or the book itself too dramatic. People hate overly dramatic characters and scenes. If you've got a bipolar individual in your book, it's okay to over-dramatize that character's personality, but to have scenes starting off where people are inexplicably screaming at each other, or placing exclamation points behind almost

25 Rules to Write By

everything said is over-dramatization and poor writing. It's understandable that you want to have some dramatic scenes, but make sure they are well written and they add to the main plot of the book. Just adding drama for the sake of adding drama may cause you to come off to your readers as a dramatic author, and you'll end up getting bad reviews from good writers. Their reviews may be labeled as being better written than your book. Sure, add dramatic scenes, funny characters, villains, passive characters, aggressive characters, passive-aggressive characters, and any type of character personality you want to add, but make sure that they add to your book and they aren't over-dramatic.

25. If you use the personality of someone you know in one of your characters, be sure to differentiate the character in your book from the character in your life. The

25 Rules to Write By

last thing you want is to face any type of lawsuit. It is better to pick personality traits from several people to create one character.

Make sure your book's character does not physically resemble any of the people you're using as templates for that character. Additionally, when mixing traits, make sure one trait compliments the other. It wouldn't be wise to take gentle and loving Uncle Larry's personality and mix it with conniving and ruthless Uncle Melvin's character. Your readers should not be conflicted as to whether they want to like a character or not. Sure, it's okay to turn a bad guy good to demonstrate a point, but just don't mix two conflicting personalities.

What's Your Writing Style?

One of the worst things an author can do is attempt to write a fictional book the same way a movie or a play is cast. In the movies, many scenes are cut out to get the movie to fit within a certain time slot, but you'll often hear viewers say, "Get the book. It's more detailed than the movie." That's because many of today's award-winning movies were inspired by books. At the same time, many new authors are often inspired by movies, and they attempt to write their stories in the same manner that scenes are cast. Read the story below and see if you can identify the problems with it:

Mark was running for his life. His wife, Stacy, was chasing him with a large butcher's knife. Stacy was angry and determined to stop Mark's abuse once and for all.

What's Your Writing Style?

Craig looked out the window to see if his ride was there. Craig was excited about going to the circus with his grandfather. He was playing a video game with his cousin, Fred, and he'd taken another break to look out of the window when he saw headlights. Grandpa Craig had finally arrived.

Mark found himself up against a wall with his furious wife standing in front of him. He was gasping for air, and with each breath, he begged for his life. "I'm sorry," said Mark. "I shouldn't have hit you, Stacy. Please don't stab me. I love you."
Stacy's eyes began to fill with tears as her fury began to subside. She remembered her children. Who would raise Craig if she killed his father and ended up in prison for Mark's murder?

The sound of the horn broke through the silence in the Jacobsen house. Craig grabbed his overnight bag and rushed out of the door.

What's Your Writing Style?

He was so excited that he forgot to put on his shoes.
----End of example.

What's wrong with this story? The problem here is called scene-jumping, or not adding scene breaks. The author has taken the readers to an event where the main character (Stacy) is chasing her husband with a butcher's knife. Suddenly, the author takes the readers back to the house where an impatient little boy is happily and anxiously waiting for his grandfather to pick him up. Of course, these two events can occur at the same time, but in a book, you should never take the readers from one scene to the next unless you add a scene break. Your readers will be on the edges of their seats as they read about Mary chasing her husband. Suddenly, throwing them into the living room of a child playing video games will only confuse them. Sure, in the movies, scene-jumping is okay because the movie producers uses scene-jumping to keep you

What's Your Writing Style?

wanting more. They want to keep you locked into the movie, anxious to see the conclusion of each event. With a book, however, you need to write the story out and play it through until there is a resolution. The only time it's good to scene-jump is if one scene or situation locks in with another scene, or if you've added a scene break.

Please look at the revised story below to see how the scenes are now united to tell a story:

Mark was running for his life. His wife, Stacy, was chasing him with a large butcher's knife. Stacy was angry and determined to stop Mark's abuse once and for all.

Meanwhile, inside the house, Craig looked out the window to see if his ride was there. Craig was excited about going to the circus with his grandfather. He was playing a video game with his cousin, Fred, and he'd taken another break to look out the window when he saw headlights. Suddenly, Craig heard his father

136

What's Your Writing Style?

screaming at his mother.

"Turn down the volume," Craig said Fred. "I think my mom and dad are fighting again." Craig gazed out the window and saw figures moving in the darkness.

As he looked at one of the figures, he realized it was his father, Mark. What was he running from, and why was he running behind that old grocery store? Didn't he realize that it was a dead end? That's when Craig saw his mother pursuing his father with a large knife in her hand.

"Call 911!" screamed Craig. "My mom is trying to kill my dad!"

The sound of an old engine suddenly got Craig's attention. It was his grandfather pulling up. As Grandpa Matthew blew the horn, an anxious Craig opened the front door and ran towards his grandfather's car. Barefoot, Craig rushed outside to tell his grandfather about his parents while Fred stayed inside to call the police.

What's Your Writing Style?

"Mom and Dad are fighting, and Mom's got a knife!" Craig screamed at his Grandpa Matthew as he exited the car.

Craig pointed in the direction he'd seen his parents running in, and Grandpa Matthew ran towards the old building, yelling for Craig to go back in the house. He could see that Mark had nowhere else to run, and he screamed at his daughter-in-law as she held the knife over her head.

Mark found himself up against a wall with his furious wife standing in front of him. He was gasping for air, and with each breath, he begged for his life.

"I'm sorry," said Mark. "I shouldn't have hit you, Stacy. Please don't stab me. I love you."

Stacy's eyes began to fill with tears as her fury began to subside. She remembered her children.

Who would raise her children if she killed their father and ended up in prison for Mark's murder? The sounds of Mark's father yelling

What's Your Writing Style?

obscenities at her sent a chilling reminder to Stacy. Mark was just like his father, and if she killed Mark, Mark's father would likely get custody of her children.

----*End of example.*

Now, as you can see, the scenes are integrated, and they now make more sense. We can justify taking the readers from the scene of the crime to the living room where Craig is anxiously awaiting his grandfather's arrival. That's because the two scenes are now linked with each other.

Again, you can also change scenes by inserting what is known as scene breaks. A scene break is an image or text inserted to indicate a change of location, time or point of view. Scene breaks are usually followed with text that indicate that the story has changed. For example, you might say, "Meanwhile, back at school..." Scene breaks are only needed when two or more scenes change within a

What's Your Writing Style?

chapter, but are not needed when a chapter ends. It can be an additional blank line, several asterisks (****), or the symbol that represents the number sight (#). Of course, you can also use imagery such as a long lines or any images that are horizontal and don't take up too much space.

Movies and plays are usually inspired by books, and what the script writers do is they cut out unnecessary scenes to shorten up the movie or play. In many cases, they will record several scenes, only to cut them out when they feel they aren't adding to the scripts. The goal for them is to shorten the movie so they can lessen the production costs. But a book is completely different from a movie or play script because a book is always more detailed. Truthfully, many authors would do better as script writers than they would do as fictional writers. At the same time, many fictional authors would do better writing children's books than they would do writing fictional

140

What's Your Writing Style?

books for adults. Children's books don't require as much detail, depth, or research as adult books. Of course, there are children's books for all age ranges, so an author could decide which age group he or she is better suited for.

Children's books and play writing are both forms of fictional writing when, of course, the accounts given are undocumented. So, the best thing to determine is what type of fictional writing is better suited for you.

Children's Books

Children's books don't usually require a lot of details because children are impatient and don't care much for details. Please review the short story below.

Joe went to the store. At the store, Joe saw Jane, and Jane was beautiful. Jane asked Joe if he'd seen her on television the night before. Joe said that he had seen Jane on television. *----End of example.*

141

What's Your Writing Style?

This writing style is better suited for children's books. If you're an author or aspiring author who's impatient and you don't like to write lengthy dialogues or in-depth plots, you may find that writing children's books is better suited for you. Children's books are normally ten to one hundred pages long, with the average book being about fifteen to thirty pages in length. Children's books are oftentimes filled with photos, so you can write a children's book in an hour, a day or a few days.

Script Writing (Movies/ Plays)

Movie and play scripts are usually filled with a lot of dialogue and character instructions. Just like adult fiction, movies and plays have to be carefully thought out, but scripts don't have to be as lengthy or as detailed as fictional books. You'll find that ninety percent of a movie or play script is character dialogue. The rest will most often be the setting (where the scene is to be shot) and notations as to what the characters feel and what the characters are doing.

What's Your Writing Style?

If you're good with dialogue, but you're not so good with talking about details, then script writing may be better suited for you than adult fiction. Check out the two short stories below:

Sandra was running through the field. She was hot, and sweat poured from her face. Her car had broken down on the side of the road. Sandra had seen a few alligators in the area, so she was afraid of being stranded on that secluded road. It was getting dark outside, so Sandra decided to run across a field nearby to reach the main highway. There, she could stop a passerby and ask them to call for help.
----End of example.

The story above isn't bad, but it's also not very detailed. Check out the extensive and more detailed story below:

The grass cut into Sandra's skin as she jogged through the thick brush; nevertheless, the pain from the cuts on her legs were the least of her

What's Your Writing Style?

worries. Even though the day was coming to an end, temperatures in Texas were still in the mid nineties, and Sandra was feeling fatigued. She took the shirt she had in her hand to wipe the sweat away from her face. She'd taken off her shirt, but she was still wearing a camisole underneath. Each step proved to be as painful as the first as the grass continued to cut away at Sandra's exposed legs. At that moment, she regretted wearing a shirt skirt to her job interview.

While on her way back to the city, her car had broken down just a few minutes after she'd driven past a few alligators. The alligators had been sitting on the banks of a nearby river. The day was coming to a close, and the sky had taken on an orange-like color. Sandra sat in her car for fifteen minutes, trying to get a signal on her cellular phone, but the high temperatures slowly turned Sandra's vehicle into what felt like a microwave.
Sweaty and fearful, Sandra knew she had to

What's Your Writing Style?

make a decision. She could either run across the brush nearby in hopes that she wouldn't run into a rattlesnake or a well-hidden alligator, or she could stay in her car in hopes that someone would find her before nightfall. The brush was a quarter of a mile long, but on the other side of the brush was a major highway. If Sandra stayed in her car, she likely wouldn't be found until the next day because the road was secluded and only known by residents who lived in that area. Most of the residents that drove down that road were elderly, and they were all more than likely in for the evening. After considering her options, Sandra decided that she would have to take her chances and run through the brush nearby.

Sandra opened her car door and got out of her vehicle. She could see the smoke still rising from the car's engine. The stench of what smelled like rusty water mixed with oil filled the air, and the sounds of crickets singing were as annoying as they were frightening. Sandra

What's Your Writing Style?

nervously rubbed her arms and shook her clothes to make sure no insects had gotten on her. She was afraid of insects.

Without warning, Sandra heard a hissing sound. She turned around to see a rattlesnake just a few feet ahead of her. The snake was coiled up and could have easily been overlooked since it blended well with the road. Sandra looked behind her and started to back up slowly. She didn't want to scare the snake with any sudden movements. After she was about ten feet away from the snake, Sandra took off running into the brush nearby. If she could only get to the main highway, she could stop a vehicle passing by, or maybe, she'd get a phone signal.

Sandra's legs felt as if they were on fire. The brush was filled with sharp blades of grass, small trees and thorny plants. The pain from each cut felt almost unbearable, but she knew she had to get to the main highway if she

What's Your Writing Style?

wanted to live. Sandra's legs felt wet, but she didn't know if the grass was wet or if she was bleeding. She didn't care. She needed to get to that highway safe and sound.

----End of example.

In the first dialogue, you can see that the writer was rushed, or it could be that the writer is writing a short story. Cutting out details is okay for short stories, but it is always better to give the readers a more detailed experience as this makes the story more engaging. If you'd prefer sample one's example more than you prefer sample two's example, you may be better at movie or play writing than you are at fictional writing for adults.

Standard Fiction for Adults

As we've already discussed throughout this book, standard fictional writing can be very lengthy and detailed. That's because, unlike children, adults don't usually have images in their books to guide their imaginations.

What's Your Writing Style?

Instead, as adults, we have the responsibility of imagining what we're reading. Sure, we can easily imagine Sandra running through the grass, but to make the story more real to us, we would need to experience Sandra running through the grass. If we didn't know that there were sharp blades, small trees, and thorny plants in the brush, our only thoughts would be of Sandra effortlessly running through a field. But now that we know that Sandra was getting cut up by the brush, and she was in a lot of pain, we are more engaged in the story. We are now vicariously running through Sandra, and we are anxiously trying to get Sandra to safety.

Fictional writing for adults is definitely more tedious, but it can also be more rewarding.

The style that's better for you will depend on your patience, your creativity, and your ability to take your thoughts and convey them in a way that your target audience can understand.

What's Your Writing Style?

Don't feel down if you're unable or unwilling to put the necessary time and effort into a fictional book. Instead, focus on what you can do and are willing to do for now. It is better to write a play or a children's book than it is to push out a poorly written fictional book for adults.

If you want to write fictional books, even though you don't have the patience or gifting to do so, don't fret. There are people out there who you can hire to read your books and give you pointers along the way. If you're willing to take critique, and if you're willing to invest the time and money needed to clean up your book, you will likely publish a book with best-seller potential. Always remember that most best-selling authors were once poor writers who kept investing in their skill or gifting until they got the knowledge and understanding they needed to become best-sellers. In other words, they didn't give up, and neither should you. Criticism is nothing more than a dividing line that separates the fearful from the fearless.

Writing a Best-Seller

Of course, it is every author's dream to become a best-selling author. People don't write books just to read them in the privacy of their own homes; people write books to express themselves and their views. But most people aren't exceptional writers, nor is the average person patient enough to put together a best-selling novel or short story. Oftentimes, poor writing can be summed up in three words: Lack of knowledge.

If you don't know better, you won't do better. When someone reads your book, they will see how much of yourself that you put into that book. Were you passionate about what you wrote, or were you just determined to write a book because your cousin wrote a book? Believe it or not, your state of mind when you write a book will always reveal itself to your

Writing a Best-Seller

readers. For this reason, your books should be full of creative thinking, love, passion, and useful information.

Your reputation is your face of success, and you want to keep it as spotless as possible. Bad reviews are like scratches obtained in a fight, and the more you receive, the worse you'll look. A lot of writers don't think about the reviews; they are just anxious to write and finish their books.

Books are like buildings. How you build them and what you choose to build them with will determine their value. With that being said, your book should have the following building blocks:

* **A plot.** A book without a plot is a book without a chance. Your plot will take your readers from point A to point B, but at the end of it all, your readers expect to reach an exciting and thought-provoking climax.

Writing a Best-Seller

* **Realistic characters.** If your readers cannot relate to the characters, they won't enjoy your book. Additionally, if your characters sound scripted, your readers won't be able to relate to them; therefore, they'll label your book a bad read.

* **Vivid descriptions.** Readers expect to read detailed descriptions of the characters, character movements, character feelings, locations and so on. For example, if you write a story saying that your character is standing outside in below freezing temperatures, you should also detail how your character feels. Don't just say that the character is cold; that's obvious, but make the readers feel as if they are in that very place. A great way to express how the character feels is to describe the climate and talk about the character's bodily mishaps (goosebumps, runny nose, or frostbite).

Writing a Best-Seller

*   **Suspense.** The most boring of books are books that read as if they were written by a cactus. You can't give the story away immediately; you have to make your readers try to figure things out on their own, and end up getting it wrong several times. Suspense is what keeps the readers interested in your book.

*   **A climax.** How would you feel if you climbed a mountain only to realize that there is no peak? How would you feel if you dove into a river only to find out that there is no depth? That's what a reader feels when they come to the end of a book only to find out there is no climax. Suspense sets the reader up for the climax, but if you end a book without explaining the content of that book, you've just ticked off a lot of people.

Best-sellers aren't just written; they are built. You can't just throw a bunch of words together

Writing a Best-Seller

and expect it to become a best-seller. People like to walk away entertained and informed. In addition, human beings are emotional creatures, and best-sellers often activate all of their emotions. Your readers won't mind you causing them to feel sad if the book goes on to make their sadness feel somewhat justified. Towards the close of your book, the joy and revelation you give to your readers must exceed every depth of sadness or anger that you took those readers into. For example, if you tell a story about Grady losing his wife and children to a freak accident, losing his job because of an insensitive boss, and losing his friends because he refused to drop a lawsuit, you'd better give Grady a victory in court. You'd also need to give Grady another wife or potential wife, more children, or at least show that Grady's new wife is pregnant, and better friends before you end that book. Simply saying that Grady won the lawsuit, and then closing the book with "the end" is a sure-fire way to disappoint a bunch of hopeful readers.

Writing a Best-Seller

If Grady walks away with nothing but money, your readers will give your reputation a well-deserved black eye.

Don't give up if your first book isn't a hit. This is normal, and it doesn't mean you're a poor writer. Just keep writing and you'll get better and better as you go along. You'll also acquire more readers as you go along. Below are a few more tips to help you on your writing journey.

1. Always go back and reread your book from an objective point of view. Print the book, take it away from your writing station, and read the book the same way you'd envision someone else would read it. Make sure you take a pen with you to strike through the errors that you see.

2. Hire an editor. A lot of authors don't realize the importance of hiring an editor, so they try to save a few hundred

Writing a Best-Seller

or a few thousand bucks and publish
their books as they are. Five years
later, they've only sold twenty books,
and gotten ten bad reviews. You may
think that misspelled words,
grammatical errors or poor sentence
structure is something your readers
should just overlook, but the average
reader will stop reading once they run
into a few errors. That's because they
will feel like they paid for a flawed
product.

3. Hire someone to critique your book.
   Sure, a critique may hurt your feelings,
   but if it isn't published, it won't do you
   any extensive harm. A bad review, on
   the other hand, may just cause you to
   retire your writing pen. You can find
   affordable developmental editors online
   to critique your book.

4. Research... Research... Research. The
   more you know, the more you can write.
   You shouldn't limit the characters in your

Writing a Best-Seller

books to only the professions and lifestyles you're familiar with. If you make character Stephanie a heart surgeon, you would need to research the things that Stephanie may say in and outside of the hospital. For example, if Stephanie is dating Daniel, what would Stephanie say to Daniel if she were describing an operation she'd performed earlier? You would need to make Stephanie read as a knowledgeable doctor.

5. Learn new words. An author with an extremely limited vocabulary is like a college professor with a fifth grade education. Authors are wordsmiths, and as such, we have to always learn new words and incorporate those words into our books as well as our vocabularies.

6. Keep it natural. Sometimes, authors write unnatural-sounding dialogues. This is usually done by authors who simply want to sound "smart". For example,

Writing a Best-Seller

let's say that you are writing a plot
where Daniel and Stephanie are having
a conversation.

Daniel asked, "Hey Stephanie. Where have
you been?"

Stephanie responded, "Today, I journeyed to
the store to acquire some potatoes. What did
you do today?"

----End of example.

Look at Stephanie's line. Who, in their *right*
mind, says that they've "journeyed" to the store
to "acquire" some potatoes? The better way is
the natural way.

Daniel asked, "Hey Stephanie. Where have
you been?"

Stephanie responded, "Today, I went to the
store to buy some potatoes. How about you?"

----End of example.

7. Keep it to the point. Don't add pointless
text or dialogue. Stay with the plot, build

Writing a Best-Seller

the suspense, and intensify the climax.

Daniel: Hey Stephanie. Where have you been?

Stephanie: Today, I went to the store to buy some potatoes. How about you?

Daniel: Nothing. Man, my leg is itching.

Stephanie: Really? That's weird. My leg was itching earlier.

----End of example.

What's the point of Daniel and Stephanie talking about their itching legs? What does this do for the story?

8. Keep it holy. Let's not forget that you're writing a Christian book. I've run across Christian authors who didn't want to accept that their books were nothing more than soft porn. Always remember to make sure that the stories and the advice in your books glorifies GOD.

9. Revise... Revise and delete! Sure, it's pretty hard to consider deleting pages of text when you've put so much work into

Writing a Best-Seller

it, but it's better to get rid of the text than to get rid of the potential readers.
Reread your book, and remove anything that does not add to the plot or direction of your book. Also, revise the text when necessary. Think of your book as a rose. You will need to prune away the dead text so your book can thrive.

10. Accept criticism and grow from it. In my line of work, I've run across a few authors who did not want to be corrected or have their books critiqued. So, when I'd edited their books, they rejected the changes, and published their books as they were. Needless to say, they didn't sell too many copies of their books. If you're a first-time author, listen to the seasoned authors. To you, your book may read like a best-seller, but a seasoned author will see your book through experienced eyes.

Exercising Your Writing Skills

When I was a new writer, I was too cheap to hire editors. I remembered that I was always good in English and Literature, so I assumed I was a superb writer. My books were filled with tasteless humor and failed attempts at being witty. Some of the things I said were disgusting, to say the least. After having a few misspelled words and grammatical errors pointed out to me in my published books, I realized just how badly I needed editors.

By the time I'd hired an editor, I had already written and published about four or more books, so my writing had gotten a little better, but not that much better. That's because I didn't have anyone to critique me. When the editor sent my (partial) book file back to me, I

Exercising Your Writing Skills

was horrified. It was obvious that she did not like my book or my wit. She was a retired school teacher, so she left me a lot of negative feedback that made me feel as if I was in grade school once again.

I remember her saying repeatedly throughout the book, "I'm not going to tell you this again." I was baffled. I'd just gotten half of the book back for the first time, so, I didn't understand her saying "I'm not going to tell you this again." My book was so draining to her that she took my money, kept promising to send me my book file back, and then, the teacher ran away with my money, teaching me a much needed lesson. I was upset, but not too mad because I'd found her via Google, went onto her website and hired her on the spot because she was a retired school teacher. At the same time, her negative feedback and her unwillingness to complete my book forced me to go back and take a look at my book. After all, I'd never reread it.

164

Exercising Your Writing Skills

As I reread my book, I was horrified. The book was a little over a year old by then, and as I mentioned before, I'd written more books after that, but I'd never published that particular book. After reading the entire book, I put it back aside because I couldn't stand reading it. There were a lot of great points in the book, but there was a lot of flesh in that book too, and it stunk real bad. Now that I edit books, I can truly understand the runaway editor's frustration.

A year later, I went back through the book, deleted pages and pages of text, rewrote some of the book, edited some of the text, and I sent it to another editor. The new editor critiqued a few lines, I made the necessary corrections, and I published a well-written book. Did I want to publish the book when I thought it was poorly written? Yes and no. I wanted to publish it because I was anxious to get it out there, but I knew that I had to put more work into that book if I wanted it to help someone.

Exercising Your Writing Skills

After that experience, I started paying more attention to my writing, reading articles about writing, and paying attention to my editors' notes. My writings began to improve, my books started selling and I eventually started teaching writing classes. Now that I teach, publish, and edit, I am passionate about seeing books written in excellence. When editing poorly written books, I get frustrated and there are times that I want to refund the authors, but I've come to understand my role in making their books better. Needless to say, I do come across a few authors here and there who aren't willing to receive developmental critiques or feedback. They simply want to be told that their books are great.

Months or years later, they'll contact me asking why their books aren't selling, and I have to tell them, once again, that their books are poorly written. Because they didn't believe me the first time, they didn't exercise or grow their writing skills. Instead, they announced to the world that they were authors, and they waited

Exercising Your Writing Skills

in vain for buyers, only to get a few buys from supportive family members and friends. They didn't want the critiques because they were anxious to publish their books. Many of them were first-time authors and they were anxious to wear the author label. Unfortunately, many authors retired from writing after publishing their first books because they didn't receive a lot of sales or recognition from their books. They simply gave up too easily.

It doesn't matter how good you were in English class, or how you fared in writing contests, you have to develop yourself as a writer. You won't be perfect the first time. As a matter of fact, as you continue your writing journey, you'll go back and reread your first and second book, and you'll likely feel ashamed or disgusted by what you've written. That's because you will be a mature and seasoned author by then, and you'll notice your writing mistakes.

Think back to the second and third grade,

Exercising Your Writing Skills

when your teacher was attempting to teach you multiplication. If you were like most seven and eight-year-old children, you found yourself getting frustrated, maybe even crying when your teacher handed you your graded lesson. The paper was likely covered in red ink, and to make matters worse, your seemingly heartless teacher placed a big sad face at the top of your paper. You were angry at your teacher because you thought that she was picking on you. As time went on, however, you got better and better at multiplication, until one day, you realized that you could multiply without counting your fingers. The point is: You got better.

Your writing journey is similar to your journey through grade school. You will almost always start off as a rookie writer, but if you don't give up, and you allow negative critiques to make you a better writer, you may eventually join the ranks of some of today's best-sellers. In the meantime, there is something you can do to

Exercising Your Writing Skills

develop your writing skills. Below are ten
pointers that will help you to become a better
writer.

1. **Write as often as you can.** The more
   you write, the better you'll become at
   writing. Start a blog or sign up to write
   for a blog or news site. When I was still
   somewhat new, I signed up to write for
   Examiner and Yahoo. I can truly go
   back and see how my writings have
   improved from 2009 until now. Writing a
   blog or writing for a news site will not
   only help you to develop your writing
   skills, but it'll help you to acquire more
   readers.

2. **Read as often as you can.** I didn't
   realize how distasteful my wit sounded
   until I edited a book full of wit. After
   editing that author's book, I reopened
   my own book and started mercilessly
   deleting pages. Sometimes, you won't
   see what you're doing wrong until you
   see someone else making that same

Exercising Your Writing Skills

mistake.

Read some books written by best-sellers so you can get a better understanding of what readers want, and read some books that have gotten a lot of bad reviews, so you can get a better understanding of what readers do not want.

3. **Get out as often as you can.** It's amazing how the things and people in this earth can inspire a book without saying a word. Go out to eat, go to the zoo, take slow strolls through your neighborhood; just get out of the house!

4. **Never run from critics; run to them!** Now, let's be real. Some critics are just critical people who shouldn't be taken seriously, but some critics are perfectionists who simply have no tolerance for poorly written books. How can you tell the difference? Review their reviews. Go to Amazon.com and check out some of the books they've reviewed. Click on their names on the Amazon

Exercising Your Writing Skills

site, and you'll see every review they've ever left. If they tend to be overly critical and rarely give good reviews, that's not a critic; that's a crybaby. Look for critics who have given as many good reviews as they have bad reviews. Also, look at the review ratings on the books that they've given bad reviews to. If most of the reviewers gave good reviews, but that particular critic is in the bottom ten percent of bad reviews, you may not want to inquire of them because they may be negative souls. Negative people read books expecting the worst, and most of their positive reviews are done just to offset their negative reviews.

5. **Learn a new word everyday**, and every time you hear a word spoken that you do not understand, look it up. We're authors, so words are our fuel. Without many words, we can't go very far. Limiting yourself to the words you

Exercising Your Writing Skills

currently know is the same as limiting yourself as a writer. Remember this rule of thumb: Hear a word, define a word. Don't be ashamed because of the words you don't understand. Oftentimes, we'll hear words, but never think to define them because we don't use them in our own vocabularies. We will have a general understanding of what they mean, but we won't have a full understanding of what they mean. Look them up, and then, incorporate them into your vocabulary. If you don't speak them, it'll be hard for you to write them.

6. **Sell your words.** There are a lot of people out there who aren't wordsmiths, so they'll pay you to write their biographies, resumes, website content, and the list goes on and on. You may not be the best writer as of yet, but you have to get practice somewhere. A lot of people don't want to pay professional writers to write their website content,

172

Exercising Your Writing Skills

bios, and resumes. Instead, they look for people who sell those services at a cheaper rate and are decent enough with words to write content that others can understand. This is where you come in. You can charge low until you begin to grow as a writer, but as your writing skills get better, your writing fees should increase.

7. **Embrace the "big word" revolution.** It's okay to use bombast words if you're writing to an audience who can understand them. Just make sure you know your target audience before you do so. If your vocabulary is extensive, you'll be a versatile writer, and therefore, you won't be limited to a certain audience.

8. **Study your Bible.** You're a Christian writer, and it would definitely help if you knew scriptures. Sure, you'll be copying and pasting scriptures, but you'll also spend a lot of time reiterating what the

Exercising Your Writing Skills

Bible says. Additionally, the Bible is full of words that you wouldn't ordinarily pay attention to; therefore, to understand some of the things said, you will have to research them. It's amazing how much clarity, knowledge and understanding you'll obtain through research.

9. **Write poetry.** Poems will always stretch you as a writer because they force you to be creative. You can't just open a document and write a poem; poems require a lot of thought and research. Practice your poetry writing skills, and you can even post up your poems at www.poetry.com. The site has a lot of poets who are willing (and sometimes required) to review the poems of others. This is a great place to get feedback, and read poetry written by others.

10. **Watch a lot of movies.** You'll learn a lot by listening to character dialogues and seeing the plots unfold in each movie. Look at how good the actors do

Exercising Your Writing Skills

their jobs, and at the same time, check out some pretty bad acting jobs. You can Google them. Learn what's good and not so good by watching others.

Writing Exercises

If you want to become a better writer, you have to practice writing. Of course, it's not fun to write material that you can't use, but it's far better than writing and paying for bad books that no one will read.

Below, you'll find ten incomplete stories. Take those stories and add your spin to them. You can even change the names of the characters to make your story more personal to you. Remember, you're a Christian writer, so make sure your rendition of every one of these stories gives GOD the glory. Also, please note that you cannot publish or profit from these stories. They are simple activities to help you become a better writer.

Writing Exercises

Story #1

Geneva made her way to the front of the church. Today was the day she'd chosen to finally give her life to the LORD. With her pantyhose ruined and one of her shoes in her hand, she limped down the aisle towards the altar. Many of the onlookers clapped as she made her way towards the pulpit.

Assignment

Finish the short story above using the follow questions as your guide:

1. Why did Geneva finally decide to give her life to the LORD? What happened to encourage this change?
2. Why was her pantyhose ruined?
3. Why was one of her shoes in her hand? Why didn't she just put the shoe back on her foot?
4. What happened when Geneva finally reached the altar?
5. How has Geneva's life changed since she gave her life to the LORD?

Writing Exercises

Story #2

Wilson was ashamed. His secret was finally out, and now, he knew he'd likely lose his job, his wife, and his children. He lowered his head as twin brother William covered his mouth in dismay.

William was ashamed of Wilson for the first time in his life. He'd always known his brother was somewhat selfish, but he had no clue Wilson could be so cold and calculating.

"I'm done," said William. "Don't call me anymore! I'm done!"

Assignment

Finish the short story above using the follow questions as your guide:

1. What did Wilson do that jeopardized his family and his career?
2. Why was Wilson ashamed?
3. Why didn't William want anything else to do with his brother?
4. Describe the conversation between Wilson and his wife? What happened

Writing Exercises

after their conversation?

5. How did Wilson ever get back in his brother's good graces?

Story #3

The sound of wolves nearby made Ross tremble, but he knew he had to remain strong for his wife, Karen. The freezing winds seemed to get worse as nightfall approached. How would they survive yet another night without being rescued?

Ross placed his arms around his wife's frail body. She was growing weaker, and Ross could tell she wouldn't survive another twenty-four hours if they weren't rescued.

"Baby, it's going to be okay," said Ross.

"We've prayed, and now, all we can do is trust GOD. Just hold on for me. Okay?"

Karen tried to lift her head, but she was too weak. She managed to open her mouth and let out a muffled okay.

Writing Exercises

Ross lifted his head to the heavens once again. "GOD, please don't let us die out here. Please send help fast." Ross's voice quivered as he continued his prayer. "I love and adore you, precious GOD, and I trust you with our lives. Please send help before daybreak." Before Ross could finish praying, he saw what appeared to be the light from a flashlight.

Assignment

Finish the short story above using the follow questions as your guide:

1. Where are Ross and Karen stranded at?
2. How did the couple come to be stranded?
3. How long would you say the couple has been stranded, and what have they done to survive?
4. Who was holding the flashlight?
5. How were the couple rescued? Give details.

Writing Exercises

Story #4

Jacqueline tilted her head back a little further. With a sweep of her hands, she moved her bangs over once again so Rachel could finish applying her mascara.

Rachel was a cosmetologist, and even though she was infamous for her lack of patience, she was the best cosmetologist in town, and she knew it. "Tilt your head back a little more," said Rachel. "I can't work with you if you don't work with me."

Jacqueline was growing restless. The pain in her neck was almost unbearable, but she knew she would have to endure the pain just a little while longer because Jacqueline was..............

Assignment

Finish the short story above using the follow questions as your guide:

1. Tell the story that led to Jacqueline coming to Rachel.
2. Describe both Jacqueline and Rachel in vivid detail.

Writing Exercises

3. Why does Rachel have such a bad attitude? Tell her story.

4. Finish the last line in the paragraph. Why did Jacqueline have to endure the pain a little while longer?

5. Humble Rachel. Use your writing skills to humble Rachel, but make sure the stories remain linked.

Story #5

Officers approached the vehicle with their guns drawn. The high speed chase was finally over after thirty minutes.

Officer Winbush yelled for the vehicle's occupant to step outside the vehicle, but there was no response. The sounds of the police helicopter drowned out the sounds of the police radios. "Driver, get out of the car now with your hands where I can see them!" screamed Officer Winbush.

Suddenly, the car door opened. The officers

Writing Exercises

positioned themselves behind their vehicles as they waited for the driver to step out. The officers could see the driver's hands, and slowly, the driver emerged from the vehicle and everyone was amazed. The officers lowered their pistols as they realized.....

Assignment

Finish the short story above using the follow questions as your guide:

1. What event caused the high speed chase?
2. Describe the high speed chase in vivid details.
3. Why were the officers amazed when the vehicle's occupant stepped out of the vehicle? Who was the occupant?
4. What did the officers realize after the vehicle's occupant stepped outside of the vehicle?
5. Describe what happened next.

Writing Exercises

Story #6

The odor in the room was almost unbearable. The loud television, the sound of babies crying, and the horrid stench was beginning to get to Katie. Nevertheless, Katie continued to hold her breath. The interview would be over in fifteen minutes, and Katie was watching the clock.

The temp agency had sent Katie to Lillian Grayson's house, and even though Katie had heard about the house most people referred to as the Devil's Nest, she knew she could not miss this interview. After all, the temp agency required all registrants to apply for every job they'd recommended to them; otherwise, the temp agency could reject their applications for employment.

This was Katie's last interview of the day, and she was more than anxious to get home and try to shower off the stench of Mrs. Grayson's home.

"Excuse me, for a moment" said Lillian as she stood to her feet and went towards her

Writing Exercises

bedroom.

While Lillian was in the other room, Katie began to search the room with her eyes. Clothes were strewn about everywhere. There were children's toys, paperwork, and even open containers of what appeared to be old food lying around the room. As Katie looked around, she found herself swatting at a couple of flies that had obviously found her interesting. *LORD, please don't let this lady hire me,* Katie thought to herself. At that moment, Lillian emerged from the back room carrying a piece of paper.

"You're hired!" she said with a large smile. Katie was horrified. What had she done right? She didn't want to work for the Graysons. Just as she was about to speak, a little movement behind Ms. Grayson caught her eyes. It was a dying fish lying on the counter.

Assignment
Finish the short story above using the follow

186

Writing Exercises

questions as your guide:

1. Why was Katie unemployed? What happened to her previous job?

2. When the temp agency told Katie that she would be interviewing with Mrs. Lillian Grayson, describe her reaction. List a dialogue no less than ten lines long between Katie and Mr. Ulysses, the temp agency's manager.

3. Describe Katie's home life and her goals.

4. Why was the Grayson's home referred to as the Devil's Nest?

5. What happened after Lillian told Katie that she had the job? How did Katie respond? Did she take or refuse the job? How did her choice affect her at the temp agency?

Story #7

"Nooooooooooo! Leave me alone! You're not my Daddy! Stop! You're not my Daddy!"

Writing Exercises

It was obvious to Frank that Evan was having yet another nightmare. This was the third night in a row that he'd dreamed about some guy saying that he was his dad.

The disappointment in Frank's eyes was evident. He'd just settled in after working a long day, and he was about to eat the buffalo wings his wife, Natalie, had left for him on the stove. He was also about to watch the recorded football game, but it seemed that tonight would be another long night.

Frank stood to his feet and made his way into his son's room. Evan was sweating profusely. "Stop it! You're not my Dad! Stop!" screamed Evan.

Frank placed his hand on Evan's shoulder and gently nudged him.
"Evan? Evan? Wake up. You're having a bad dream," said Frank.

Evan sat up startled. He looked at his dad and

Writing Exercises

began to wipe his eyes.

"Go to the bathroom and pee," said Frank.
"And then, come and tell me about your
dream."

Evan stared confusingly at Frank for a minute
before getting out of his car-shaped bed.
Once Evan came back into the room, he
walked up to his dad and extended his arms.
He wanted Frank to pick him up so he could
tell him about his nightmare.

"Daddy? The bad man came back and he said
he was my dad," said Evan. "He was trying to
take me from Mom, but Mom told him to leave
us alone."

Evan's words baffled Frank. Leave *us* alone?
Curious, Frank decided to pry a little more.
"Have you seen this man before when you
weren't dreaming?" asked Frank. "Like, have
you seen him in real life?"

Writing Exercises

Evan nodded his head.

"He was at the store the other day, and I heard him tell Mom that he was my Dad. I told him he wasn't my Dad."

Frank's eyes got bigger as he sat Evan back on his bed. Could this man be the same one he'd seen his wife arguing with at her job a couple of times?

"What did your Mom tell you about the man?" asked Frank.

Evan grabbed his teddy bear and started to play with it.

"Evan, tell me what your Mom said about the man. I won't be mad at you," said Frank.

Evan kept his eyes on his teddy bear for a couple of minutes. Finally, he laid the toy back down and turned to his father. With his head lowered, Evan whispered, "It was a guy from her job. The guy was mad at Mommy and he

Writing Exercises

said that he was my dad. He said that he was
going to take me from Mommy, but Mommy
was crying and yelling at him. Mommy asked
him to be quiet, and she told me not to tell you
what the man said. She said that you would be
mad at her."

Assignment

Finish the short story above using the follow
questions as your guide:

1. Let's say that this is the beginning of the
    story. Give the viewers a flashback of
    the confrontation between Natalie and
    her co-worker.
2. Give a detailed account of the prior two
    dreams Evan had. Why hadn't he told
    his father about Natalie's co-worker
    then? What had he said to his father?
3. List five things Frank's wife previously
    did to arouse his suspicions about her
    and her co-worker. Be as detailed as
    possible.
4. Describe the confrontation that Frank

Writing Exercises

and his wife will have when Natalie returns home from work the following morning.

5. Determine Evan's paternity, and list the events that occurred after the revelation.

Story #8

Pastor Barksdale pulled into the church's parking lot. It was three o'clock in the morning and he was determined to catch whoever it was that had been breaking into his church for the last five weeks. It seemed that the police weren't doing much, and the good pastor had decided to take matters into his own hands.

Previously, Wayne Barksdale told the officers that he believed the break-ins were occurring anywhere between twelve and three in the morning since he normally left the church every night around nine, and the street the church was located on was usually pretty busy until midnight. He had also informed the officers

Writing Exercises

that he normally arrived at the church between four-thirty and five o'clock every morning, and that's how he was able to project the time slot he believed that the break-ins occurred. After filling out numerous police reports, the pastor had given up hope that the police would ever catch the burglar.

As Pastor Barksdale approached the church, he noticed what appeared to be the light from a candle emitting through one of the stain-glassed windows. His heart raced as he considered the possibilities of what he would find and what would happen to him. After all, he'd went out to the church while his wife was asleep because she'd previously rebuked his idea about going to the church in the middle of the night to catch the burglar himself. But, now, here he was standing at the door inserting the key into the knob.

In a fast motion, Pastor Barksdale turned the door knob, pushed the door open, and turned

Writing Exercises

the lights on. Just a few feet ahead of him sat a man who was obviously homeless. His hair was long and matched his peppery black and white beard. He wore a plaid red and black jacket, and in his hand was a plate he'd taken from the church's kitchen. The beggar looked up at Pastor Barksdale. His eyes were friendly, and the pastor didn't feel threatened by him.

Assignment

Finish the short story above using the follow questions as your guide:

1. Describe the previous burglaries.
2. Describe the escalation of the events that led up to Pastor Barksdale investigating the string of burglaries that plagued his church.
3. What happened after Pastor Barksdale ran into the burglar? Describe the event and the dialogue between the two.
4. Why had the burglar been breaking into Pastor Wayne's church? Tell the story of the burglar's life, and what led to his

Writing Exercises

homelessness.

5. Add an element of surprise. Finish this story with an event that the readers did not expect.

Story #9

Antoinette stormed into the school with her anxious little brother, Jamal, behind her and pleading with her to calm down. Antoinette was fourteen years old, and Jamal was eleven years old. Jamal screamed his sister's name as she bolted from classroom to classroom looking for Cole Sanders. Cole Sanders was the elementary school bully, and at thirteen years of age, he was older and bigger than the other children.

Jamal begged his sister to go home as she stormed down the halls toward the one place she suspected Cole would be: the school's library. "Nettie, let's just go home! Please! He didn't hit me that hard, so drop it!" yelled Jamal,

Writing Exercises

but Antoinette would not listen.

By this time, a small crowd had begun to follow Antoinette. She wasn't a student at Bakersfield Elementary anymore, but it was clear she was there to fight.

One of the substitute teachers screamed Antoinette's name, but she couldn't get to Antoinette because of the crowd.

The doors of the library swung open, and Antoinette emerged with her eyes fixed on Cole. She walked into the library with one thing on her mind, and that was to give Cole Sanders a bigger black eye than he'd given her brother.

Everyone in the library stood to their feet as Antoinette charged at Cole. With little time to respond, Cole tried to cover his face, but it was too late. Antoinette unleashed a fury of blows on Cole's face that left him questioning if she was really a girl.

Knowing that Antoinette was getting the best of

Writing Exercises

him, Cole kicked Antoinette, but this move only further infuriated her. Without warning, she head-butted Cole with so much force that Cole fell to the floor conscious, but beaten.

The Principal broke through the crowd and picked up Antoinette, making sure to lock her arms, but she had done what she'd set out to do. She'd sent a message to Cole Sanders that attacking her brother was not a smart move. Jamal's bully was lying on the floor with a lump on his head that eventually earned him the nickname the Unicorn.

Assignment

Finish the short story above using the follow questions as your guide:

1. Describe the events that led up to Antoinette attacking Cole.
2. What happened to Antoinette after the fight? Remember, she was trespassing because she was no longer a student at Bakersfield Elementary.

Writing Exercises

3. Arrange a parent to parent conference between Antoinette and Jamal's parents with Cole's parents. How did it go?
4. Three days after the fight, Cole returned to school with a large lump on his head. Describe the students' reactions, and describe how Cole felt.
5. What happened to Jamal after this fight? Did Cole ever bother him again?

Story #10

Ethan readjusted his suit as he prepared to meet Talib, a Kenyan warrior and leader of a small tribe or rebels called the Umpitsu. Ethan had been in Kenya investigating what he'd believed to be illegal trade operations between some prominent Congressmen and the Umpitsu. He believed that some of the Congressmen were trafficking a powerful new sedative known as Buniyak into the United States.

According to Ethan's research, Buniyak was

Writing Exercises

derived from a small plant called the Bunipulus, and this small, but potent plant was responsible for the deaths of more than five thousand Kenyans. He had what he believed to be solid evidence that some members of the United States Congress were trafficking Buniyak, and using it to contaminate some of the water in his city.

News reports had stated that more than thirteen college students had become sick after drinking water from a fountain at Emarion College, and Ethan was sure that Buniyak was to blame for those incidents. He wasn't sure why they wanted to poison the water, but he knew that he needed to do something to stop them.

Ethan also believed that Congressman Lloyd Pridgett's frequent trips to Kenya proved that he was the mule that the other Congressmen used to traffic the plant.

After visiting a few villages in the mountains of Mogila, Ethan had learned the location of the

Writing Exercises

Umpitsu, and he'd traveled into the heart of what was referred to as Umpitsu country. While in the land, Ethan had been kidnapped by Umpitsu warriors who'd been tipped off about his investigations. As it turned out, the Umpitsu had more power than Ethan had anticipated.

The warriors that kidnapped Ethan took him into what appeared to be a large cave. Ethan's heart raced as he made his way further and further into the cave, not knowing what to expect. The warriors took Ethan to a room where one of the tribe's priests came in and began to speak with him.
Ethan was amazed at how well the priest spoke English. The priest informed Ethan that Talib, the tribe's leader, would come out to meet with him soon.
Ethan heard a knocking that was so loud that the warriors who had him in their custody became distracted long enough for him to attempt his escape, but he didn't get far. The

Writing Exercises

warriors wrestled Ethan to the ground, and the priest held his legs as he attempted to free himself.

Suddenly, a door opened and in came a man with a needle in his hand. The warriors were gone and Ethan realized that he was yet again being restrained by the doctors at Saint Meritus Asylum. Doctor Slovoski made his way to Ethan, and stuck the needle into his neck. After that, Ethan felt his body relax even though his mind and heart were still racing. Ethan slowly drifted off to sleep, and peace was restored at the asylum yet again. The reality was: Ethan was schizophrenic.

Assignment

Finish the short story above using the follow questions as your guide:

1. Tell the story of Ethan's life before he entered the asylum, but from Ethan's point of view. Remember, Ethan's reality is distorted by schizophrenia.

2. Create the news report that Ethan

Writing Exercises

allegedly read about the deaths of more than five thousand Kenyan because of the Buniyak drug.

3. Why did Ethan believe Congress was tainting the water in his city? Create a few scenarios and build up the readers' suspicions as well. (The readers should not know that Ethan is schizophrenic until the end of the book. They should believe Ethan, sympathize with him, and then, find out that Ethan was ill later on.

4. Cause Ethan to confront one of the Congressmen in reality. Take Ethan to an event and cause him to publicly and loudly confront the Congressman.

5. What happened to Ethan after the drugs wore off? Send him back to the Umpitsu vision, and cause him to meet with Talib.

Continue to create stories like these over time. Write some of them down, and create some mentally. Just play around with ideas and try not to be too boring. Jot some of your ideas

Writing Exercises

down as soon as get them, because you'll find that a good idea only sticks around for a few minutes before running off to become someone else's good idea.

Practice often and never give up. Remember this: There are many pretty decent writers with great potential in this world, but they've told themselves that they aren't good writers. After writing one or two books, they gave up and learned how to do whatever their jobs required them to do. Then again, there are some really bad writers with seemingly no potential in this world, but they told themselves that they were great writers. After writing a few books and receiving a lot of criticism, they actually became great writers, and eventually, they became best-sellers.

Oftentimes, great writers read good material and swear they can do better, but the world will never know if this is true or not because they're too afraid to be who GOD has created them to be. Don't let this be the story that someone

Writing Exercises

tells about your life one day.